MW00909344

WHAT ARE YOU AFRAID OF?

WHAT ARE YOU AFRAID OF?

BY MICHAEL HYDE

2005 WINNER, KATHERINE ANNE PORTER PRIZE IN SHORT FICTION

University of North Texas Press
Denton, Texas

©2005 Michael Hyde

All rights reserved.
Printed in the United States of America.

10 9 8 7 6 5 4 3 2 1

Permissions:
University of North Texas Press
P.O. Box 311336
Denton, TX 76203-1336

The paper used in this book meets the minimum requirements of the American National
Standard for Permanence of Paper for Printed Library Materials, z39.48.1984. Binding
materials have been chosen for durability.

Library of Congress Cataloging-in-Publication Data

Hyde, Michael, 1973-
  What are you afraid of? / by Michael Hyde.
     p. cm. — (Katherine Anne Porter Prize in Short Fiction series ; no. 4)
  ISBN-13: 978-1-57441-201-7 (pbk. : alk. paper)
  ISBN-10: 1-57441-201-9 (pbk. : alk. paper)
  1. Pennsylvania—Social life and customs—Fiction. 2. Alienation (Social psychology)—
Fiction. I. Title. II. Series.

  PS3608.Y37W47 2005
  813'.6—dc22

                    2005017593

What Are You Afraid Of ? is Number 4 in the Katherine Anne Porter Prize in
Short Fiction Series

This is a work of fiction. Any resemblance to actual events or establishments or to
persons living or dead is unintentional.

Text design by Carol Sawyer/Rose Design

The secret of man,—the sower.
The secret of woman,—the soil.
My secret: Under a mound that you shall never find.

—Edgar Lee Masters, *Spoon River Anthology*

contents

acknowledgments

I am indebted to many whose wisdom, nourishment, and support contributed to these stories and my life with them: Andy Augusto, Diana Cavallo, Michael Cunningham, Karen DeVinney, Thea Diamond, Wesley Gibson, Mary Gordon, Maureen Howard, Christie Hyde, Gary Hyde, Susan Hyde, Anna Jakobsson, Buboo Kakati, Jill Lamar, Romulus Linney, Vicki Moss, Joyce Carol Oates, Margaret Penney, Otto Penzler, Barbara Rodman, Justin Rogers-Cooper, Raymond Smith, Nat Sobel, Ronald Spatz, Sharon Oard Warner, and Don Williams.

I also wish to thank these publications, in which some of the stories in this collection originally appeared, often in slightly or very different form:

"Her Hollywood" in *Alaska Quarterly Review* and reprinted in *The Best American Mystery Stories 2001*.

"People's Choice" in *Ontario Review*.

"What Is Now Proved Was Once Only Imagined" in *New Millennium Writings*.

"Miracle-Gro" in *Xconnect: Writers of the Information Age*.

"Everything Valuable and Portable" in *Mars Hill Review*. This copyrighted story was originally published in *Mars Hill Review*, a 200-page journal of essays, studies, and reminders of God. For more information, please contact 1-800-990-MARS or visit www.marshillreview.com.

"Second-Hand" in the *Austin Chronicle* online and reprinted in *The Trace*.

"Life Among the Bulrushes" in *Bloom*.

her hollywood

The girl was Mary Alice Bunt and they found her by the river. My brother Wade and I thought we'd see the print her body made but rain came and the river jumped its banks before we could find the spot. It's a good thing the search party found her when they did. She's liable to have been washed away and lost because everything came rushing in that brown flood: flat tires, TV antennas, a doll carriage like one I used to push.

Mary Alice Bunt was pretty. I know this for two reasons. The first is because her picture was front-page in both the morning and evening *Dispatch*. The next day they put her picture in the obituary section too, except smaller. The second reason I know Mary Alice Bunt was pretty is because my mother said so. Wade and I'd just come home from school and there Mom was bawling her eyes out. Her make-up wasn't smeared so I figured she hadn't been crying long. "Always the pretty ones that die," she was saying over and over, and she didn't have to say anything else because I know she was thinking I was safe as could be. Plain Jane she liked to call me, teasing me to hear me shout that my name was Constance, Connie, not stupid Jane. She got a big kick out of it and laughed like it was the joke of the century. Even when she'd let me sit down beside her at the vanity she'd start comparing our faces, hers with mine, and she'd always throw in "You can thank your father for that nose." The way she said it I knew I didn't need to be thanking anybody.

When Mom was crying about Mary Alice, Wade and I tried to give her a hug because that's what I thought she was expecting but she pushed us out of the way and started walking around the kitchen—her head bent a little bit to the side—moving like a statue would move if it could. I don't need to tell you that my mother was an actress at the community theater. She taught me and Wade from the very start about drama, which she said translated into English as meaning "larger than life." Thanks to her, Wade and I were *drama* experts. We'd have to be, the way she changed moods like clothing. Sometimes, she even claimed she could read important messages in the clouds. We all remember Mom's Mary Alice act as one of her final performances because ten days later she left us for Hollywood. It's strange how those two things happened, one right after the other, that girl dying and my mother going away.

I didn't know Mary Alice Bunt. She was three grades below me at the junior-senior high, in the sixth grade with my brother Wade. Wade didn't know her either but that was because Wade didn't know anybody. He wasn't smart about people or in general but I still loved him in the way you have to love dogs that can only stare at you when you've thrown a stick for them to fetch. At school the kids called Wade *LD*. He was in the special class for kids with *Learning Disabilities*. There were only three other LDs at our school. They had class in one room painted bright yellow over the cinderblocks. "Hey LD," kids said when they saw Wade in the hall. "Hey, LD, what's 1 + 1?" Like Mom said once: Wade's head's just not what it's supposed to be. He'll never be like other kids, no matter how hard he studies or practices or tries.

When she was alive I never would've cared who Mary Alice Bunt was. Or anyone like her. And since Wade wasn't smart about people and since I didn't care about them, he and I were always together. I'd find him each lunch period standing at the front of the cafeteria, straining his neck one-hundred-eighty degrees until he'd see me. The kids at school made fun of us both because we were together so much. Somebody saw me dragging him by the hand one time home from school, so after that everybody called us boyfriend and girlfriend and sometimes made kissing noises so loud the teachers could hear. The teachers didn't do anything and I stopped expecting they would.

Except for the kids' teasing, I didn't mind Wade. He needed somebody and I was the only somebody left. When Mom left for her Hollywood, Dad turned into a ghost and sat all the time in front of the television, watching talk shows and how-to programs on the public channel. He stopped brushing his hair. It stuck together and shot in all directions, it was so oily. He let his beard grow out too and would sit rubbing his hand across his face, making that sandpaper sound. He only moved for the bathroom. He'd make it to bed at night sometimes but usually he stretched out on the couch and cloaked himself with a ratted gray afghan. He was like an invalid, he loved Mom that much.

I tried not to notice but our house was falling apart, creaking and complaining anytime you'd move. The barn got a big hole in the roof and let in rain. Wade and I had to take care of the cows but we stopped shoveling their shit every single day. One heifer would stare at us and bawl when she couldn't find a warm place.

That's when I got the idea to look for where Mary Alice Bunt died. Finding it wasn't easy. First Wade and I tried piecing together pictures from the news and the papers. Before she was dead, Mary Alice lived in a part of Sinking Springs called Scratch Acres. The Scratch family used to own a hotel there, and that's how the place got its name. The hotel's gone now and it's nothing but cheap trailers—one lived-in box after the other—lined up along Scratch Road.

Wade and I spent whole afternoons zigzagging from our farm to Scratch and to the bridge farther down the Susquehanna. When the searching didn't work we tried talking to Scratch kids. The ones I asked acted like they never heard of Mary Alice. Her living seemed as forgettable as the plastic milk jug some were kicking around because they didn't have a ball. A part of Mary Alice—a memory I mean—had to be somewhere. After all, she'd lived her life there, under those stupid pink and yellow and green pool-party lights hung from the trailers that tried to fool you into thinking Scratch Acres was a happy place.

Mary Alice's little brother was the one finally that showed us the way. We didn't know it was him at first so he was a lucky find, sitting in the street, pushing a toy submarine across gravel. He was eight or nine and dusted white from the shale. Wade said to him, "Do you know where they found that dead girl?" and I looked at Wade queer for saying it that way but that's when the boy nodded and told us he was the dead girl's brother.

"Can you show us where they found her?" I asked.

He led us down to the river like we were visiting tourists who'd never been before. I watched the thick band of dirt around his neck when he ducked under briars and jumped over the black logs in our way. Wade had trouble keeping up because he was tall and sort of large and said a couple times that he was going to go back. "Shut up, Wade," I said. And he did.

The boy took us to a place where the river snaked hard around a bend. Three gray trees leaned at the water, their roots and the bank had been worn away so. You could tell there'd been the flood even though the high water was gone. A lawnchair with all the stringing busted out sat up straight in the shallows. In other spots fallen branches made it look like somebody'd been trying to build a bonfire the way the branches had stacked themselves. The boy ran for the chair and kicked it over into the water.

"There's where," he said. He pointed with his submarine at a small green island ten feet from the shore. He was proud to be showing us.

Wade ran ahead too and bent over the lump of land. He was wearing his cut-offs and creek-shoes and at its deepest, the water came up to Wade's knees. "I think this is where her head was. I can see her skull-print," he said.

I followed him, looked to where he meant, but he was seeing what he wanted to see, trying to impress me. His face was wrinkled and stupid with excitement. I wanted him to go away. Suddenly all I could think about was that: how I wanted to be alone. In this place where Mary Alice Bunt had spent the last seconds of her life I wanted to be by myself. The small green island, probably not much bigger than Mary Alice had been, was somehow mine.

"No, that's not it," I said. "The boy's lying."

This was all it took for Wade to shove Mary Alice's brother. "You shouldn't tell lies," Wade said. He snatched the submarine and zoomed it through the air high above the squeaking boy's head.

"Give it back to him," I said. Wade looked at me ashamed. Finally he gave the toy back then yelled after Mary Alice's brother who ran off toward Scratch.

I looked at the green island, the size of a coffin, and imagined Mary Alice there face down like the newspaper mentioned. I imagined her underwear yanked to her ankles, her shirt pulled up over her head, her goodies—as my mother called them—showing. I wanted to be alone with her. What was it like, living and dying in your pretty body? I wanted to ask.

The next day after school I told Wade I was going for a walk without him. "Why, Connie? Why?" he asked.

I told him I was sick of him hanging around all the time. I told him I needed space and that I didn't want to be his girlfriend anymore.

He was about to turn on the waterworks so I walked off quick enough so I didn't have to see. I heard him following, so I ran. "Go away! Leave me alone!"

In Scratch four kids were playing maypole with snapped clothesline and the pole it was tied to. They ducked in and out of one another's way until they tangled and ended up arguing over whose fault it'd been. I could hear the sound of the river humming just under their angry voices.

Across the street two boys my age were rolling tires around a car they'd set up on blocks. They had their shirts off so I could see the tattoos on their arms. They watched me, stopped what they were doing and watched me. I stared them straight in the eyes.

The one boy's face looked like you were supposed to see it from one side. The other half was all messed up and pushed together like it'd been smashed by a brick. His mouth had space where teeth were supposed to be and when he smiled a black nothing spread between his lips.

The other boy's face was wide open like a book and red with freckles that matched his hair. His right arm was bigger than his left. "Woo-hoo," he whistled. I just stared at him, thinking how easily he could've been the one who'd killed Mary Alice, thinking *you are the one you are the one you are the one* until the boys and their car were no longer in sight. Until I'd walked so far they disappeared along with their litterbox trailers.

I got to the spot where the river turned. The chair Mary Alice's brother kicked over was still on its side. Small crayfish scooted when my shadow came near. The only difference was that one of the three leaning trees had finally given up and fallen. Its branches speared down into the water a few feet from Mary Alice's island.

The water was cold and I could feel mud and pebbles squishing inside my creek-shoes. The water came up to my knees but I didn't care. Mary Alice's island was in front of me, so bright and green and with a single strand of blue chicory that looked more like a silk flower than real, poking up for the sun. I lay down like the island was a bed I hadn't slept in before. I could feel it resist me, me resisting it until I stopped caring about mud and dirt and resistance dropped away.

Putting together the lost-life of a pretty girl I started with her killer. Was he fat? Thin? Bald? Tall? All the men I'd ever seen flashed in my head. It was like choosing the right color to paint a room. Lighter or darker? Brown? Black? Or red? Red yes it would be red and I thought of the boy fixing the car. Not the boy with the smashed face. The pretty girl's murderer would not be so ugly. He could be plain but not so ugly as to be scary and not so scary as to make the last moments of her life unbearable.

So I thought of the red-haired boy. He was easy to make in my mind. I had him standing over me: his face dripping red gums dripping red freckles dripping. He was hurrying to undo his pants with his thin arm. He pushed me down. He told me he was going to kill me and that I might as well enjoy it. I might as well enjoy it while it lasted and ride the rest of my life out in a limousine. His hands were on me pressing together my breasts, his fingers fumbling. I was there on the point of something when he turned me over and pressed my face into the green-grass island, into the fish silt and the smell of the river and I couldn't breathe anymore. Inside my head I was screaming: "You're dead, Connie. Now you're dead."

My hands were where his hands had been and for a second my heart stopped. It wasn't a complete stop but more like my heart couldn't decide whether or not to keep on beating, like somebody waving her arms to keep balanced on a circus wire.

After that first time at the river I'd been murdered many times. And never the same murderer twice.

There was a big man covered with thick hair across his chest and down his back. Dark eyebrows lowered like feathers over his eyes.

There was a man with a hump.

A man with twisted teeth.

A man who whistled the entire time it happened.

They'd all tell me what they were going to do before they did it. They weren't horrible men as people might imagine. They were just men.

When I couldn't get to the river I'd stretch out on my bed, turning my head into the pillow and breathing it in like it was Mary Alice's island. Once Wade walked in on me when I was being murdered. It was raining. The river was so far away in the colored party-lights of Scratch. I was on my bed and waiting to die. Mr. Farris second period algebra had forced me onto my stomach right away. He held me by the hair. I knew with one flip of his wrist he could push my face into the mud and make me breathe the river into my lungs. He made me repeat again and again that I loved him, that I'd never leave him, that I'd follow him anywhere. I kept thinking of his hand clutching my hair, his gold watch wrapping his wrist just below that hand, the gold watch I had to notice every time he bent over my desk or wrote on the board. I heard that watch tick-ticking in my ears. "You're dead Connie," I started to say when he finally pushed my head into the mud.

That's when Wade walked in. I'm sure I looked strange to him, my nightgown pulled over my head, my legs swim-kicking at the bedroom air.

"Help me," I said to him, before the river found its way to my throat, before it drowned my voice.

He pulled my arms, slid the pillow from under my face, but he was too late. I told him so. "I'm dead," I said. "You let me die."

"What are you talking about Connie? What?" his breathing hard. He was staring at my breasts.

For a crazy second I started memorizing Wade's face. His fat nose. His marble-blue eyes. His open mouth that could change from pain to pleasure in a second. He'd never yet been one of my murderers. I felt him taking shape in my mind. But the more I looked at him the more impossible he seemed and I said "No." Wade couldn't be a murderer no matter how hard I imagined.

Then came word from Mother. The postcard she sent was plain white and said "GENERIC POSTCARD" on the front and on the back along with our address she'd scratched a message in big letters. She was reading for several things, she said. Quite a few "independent films," she said. "Acting is hard life," she said. She signed the card *Francine Barlowe*. Meaning her the actress. Not Francine Pratt my mother.

I got a sheet of paper and pen to write her and tell her all the things that'd happened. Like how Dad was going out nights. Or how Wade's teacher sent home that note saying he wasn't progressing like he should. Then I remembered Mom hadn't told us where she was going exactly; Hollywood was all. I looked on the postcard, thinking she'd squeezed her new address into a corner. The only thing I found was the post-mark—Norristown, PA, not Hollywood, CA—smudged over the stamp of an orange-bellied bluebird.

I shoved that postcard way back in the kitchen junk-drawer—behind the Scotch tape and screwdrivers and worn-out batteries—so no one would ever have to know about it but me.

One day, on our way home from school, Wade and I were walking along the road, kicking up gravel. We walked to school every day just so we wouldn't have to ride the bus with those Scratch kids. I was listening to him tell about how he'd been the only one left at dodgeball during gym and no matter who threw the ball he'd been quick enough to dodge it. The game couldn't start over until he was hit so this guy came running at him—into the circle where he wasn't allowed!—and blasted the ball into Wade's face. Wade got a bloody nose, had to go to the nurse, but the game kept on going. "No harm done," was what Wade's gym teacher said.

I was staring at Wade's bandaged nose and thinking how it could mean *No harm done* when Travis Moats drove up beside us and honked. Wade jumped in his skin but I'd seen Travis coming. It was hard to miss his dark green Thunderbird skulking along the empty road.

"You want a ride?" he said, wagging his hand out the window to get our attention. He was a senior at our school, the kind of person like me and Wade you passed in the hall for four years but wouldn't take notice to. The funny thing was I'd noticed him. He'd killed me before. I don't remember how he did it but I know I was staring into his pimply face and feeling his wild sideburns scratching at my skin. He had nice green eyes. Which is the main reason I chose him. His eyes made him a standout to me when he was a nobody to everybody else.

"So you want a ride?" he said again. Wade all of a sudden deaf and dumb just stared at him. Wade was afraid of older kids, especially seniors who drove their own cars. When I looked at Wade he was shaking his head at me. I knew he was saying "No no no no" inside but I told Travis "Yes."

Wade climbed into the backseat where two giant speakers spit out loud music. I looked at him in the side-mirror, could see him covering his ears, so I decided not to look anymore.

"You like Bon Jovi?" Travis said to me.

"Sure," I said though I couldn't tell a Bon Jovi from a Whitesnake, a Whitesnake from a Poison. I started to bob my head like I was into it.

Travis drove with one hand on the steering wheel, the other hand behind my shoulder, his arm propped along the back of the frontseat. I kept waiting for him to grab me but he didn't.

Travis didn't say anything the entire ride home. I figured out he smoked from all the cellophane wrappers on the floor. They crunched every time I'd move my foot. The pine air freshener hanging from the rearview had faded. The car windshield was filthy except for two half circles where the wipers had washed clean. Travis chewed at something and kept leaning out the window to spit. He would've been the worst boyfriend but as a murderer he was fine.

When he dropped Wade and me off at our lane I stalled a few minutes by the car door. Travis just kept chewing whatever it was that was in his mouth and looked straight ahead at the road.

"Do you want to say something?" he said finally. He turned his head like he was watching the words form inside me.

"I want you for a date," I told him, "but you have to ask me first."

Travis's eyebrows raised up a bit but lowered then like he was enjoying the taste of what I'd said. I could see Wade fidgeting at the side of the road. Finally Travis nodded. "Okay. How about Saturday?" he answered me, his voice thick.

"One o'clock," was all I said back, as if it were the most natural thing in the world.

When Travis drove away I knew there was no going back. Wade asked me to explain it to him but I couldn't. He'd never understand.

On Saturday Travis came only fifteen minutes late. I could tell he'd tried to doll himself up. His straggly hair was greased back and he was wearing a shirt I was sure his mother'd pressed for him. "Sorry I'm late," he said.

"No biggee," I told him and got into the car. I'd spent all morning getting ready. I wanted everything to be perfect: the short skirt, my underwear.

My father didn't even argue when I told him I was going out. Before Mom left he would've pitched a fit if he knew his fourteen-year-old daughter was going on a date with a senior, but not this new version of my father. He didn't even get up from his couch to wave good-bye. He just raised a glass of soda to his mouth, held an ice cube between his lips, then spit it back into the glass.

Wade followed me out to the car. I know he was wanting to go along or not wanting me to go at all but I said "Bye" and that was that. When Travis drove me away I could see Wade trying to hide himself behind the maple tree in our front yard.

Travis and I went mini-golfing two towns over. He was clumsy and not so good at aiming the ball. I played even worse than he did because I didn't want him to feel bad, like he was any less a man. I watched his ropy hands draw the putter back. The ball went bouncing out of bounds. Travis got frustrated and whacked the ball so hard it almost hit a woman's face. Seeing this I knew he'd be perfect.

We didn't have much to talk about so over ice cream when I told him I wanted to give him my goodies, he looked shocked. "You're crazy," he said at first.

"No I'm serious." After that he looked at me and smiled like it was what he'd been wanting all along.

I took him down to the river. To my favorite spot I told him. I didn't tell him why. He complained about getting wet. I sat on Mary Alice's island, the grass pushing up under my skirt. I could tell Travis was thinking that I only wanted kissing. He was sticking his fat tongue into my mouth and grabbing my breasts but he didn't try any of my clothes so I told him to. He started mumbling about not having a rubber.

"I don't care," I said.

That was all he needed. He dropped his pants and I could see the dark stains on his white underwear. This made me think he hadn't planned to get this far, that maybe he'd respected me. But that wasn't what I wanted. I wanted to be Mary Alice. I wanted his rough hands to touch me, to take me from me.

Soon he was rocking back and forth on top of me and it wasn't at all as I'd imagined. He was like a fish and flapping his arms like he didn't have any control. The sharp pain was there as I'd expected but he kept saying love things like "Oh Connie oh Connie."

I said to him what I knew he wanted to hear: "I'll never leave you. You're so beautiful I could never leave you."

His breathing got heavy and he whimpered. Then he altogether stopped. I felt wide and dirty and new and that's when I said it to him. "Kill me." Calm and serious. "I don't care how," though I wanted him to push my head into the island. But really who could tell killers how to kill?

"Ha-ha," he laughed.

I repeated myself and he stopped laughing. "You're one crazy girl," he said. He started to put on his clothes that were wet in places from the river.

"You have to," I said again. I didn't move from where his body had left me. I'm sure my print was pressed into the island.

"Are we gonna go?" he asked zipping his blue jeans.

I didn't move and looked at him thinking *you are the one you are the one you are the one.*

"Listen. I can't do it again if that's what you want."

"I want you to kill me."

"Come on. Get up." When I didn't he shook his head, slinging his shirt over his shoulder. "See ya," he said.

"You can't go." I grabbed him by the arm.

He jerked away. I dug in my fingernails, dragging them along his skin, leaving red scratches from his elbow to wrist. He looked at his arm, then at me, and shoved the side of my head. I fell so that my hands and chin pressed into the silt.

All I could do was lie there, my breath hard and caught in my chest like a trapped bird. I thought Travis was getting ready, wringing his hands, preparing his strength but then I heard walking, his feet shuffling across water and rock. He was leaving. My body expanded but didn't relax.

A car engine started, revving so loud it beat its way into my mother's voice who would be saying over and again—chanting almost—that always the pretty ones got killed. I tried to picture her overhanging a balcony, under hot Hollywood sun, reading for a director she might sleep with to become a star. I wanted to see her writing to me and Dad and Wade from a yellow hotel room where someone important was in her bathroom taking a shower. But she was somewhere else, somewhere in Norristown, living in a trailer maybe, reading for no one but herself.

I rolled over to face the horrible sky as the sound of Travis's car became smaller and smaller. "Murderer," I said. Like it was a proper name.

people's choice

One week before the fair, the year the locusts came thick and heavy and drummed their anthem all around Sinking Springs, Enid woke during the night with a start and sat straight up in bed. She was startled by the full sound that came spreading through the open window. In the room where shadows bent into dark corners, she could not separate the real from the dreamed; her eyes still glazed with sleep. The sound came again, louder and less shaped, more splitting, persistent. Graham was gone from beside her, and his boots that usually sat beside the bed were gone, too. The sound again. Number Nine, she thought. Number Nine who had been bloated for weeks with pregnancy. Enid could hear the old cow bawling, the night shattered and turned topsy-turvy with the sound, followed by the sweet silence that ran into the space left vacant. She drew the sheet up between her legs, thought of birth, her gaze fixed on the ceiling. Then she heard footsteps, in the kitchen below, the door shutting, the creaking of the stairs. Graham stood in the doorway to the bedroom—a solid figure against the moonlight that illuminated the hallway behind him.

"It's a miracle," he said, calm and deep, not moving. Enid pulled on her robe and followed him downstairs. She questioned him only with glances, knowing that Graham, when serious, would decide when it was time for him to speak. "Seeing is believing," is all that he said. Enid pushed her feet into a pair of barn boots and hurried after him. He had already gone back outside.

In the barn, the back stall beyond the salt lick was lit by a kerosene lamp hung from the rafters. The wet smell of night mixed with the miasma of damp straw and animal waste. Graham was leaning forward over the bottom half of the split door, his hands pushed down against the rotting boards. Enid pulled back the hair from her eyes to get a better look.

She didn't know what to say or what to believe. Any words that came to her were lost in the back of her throat, coming out as warm gasps of air. It was indeed a miracle, as Graham had said, the newly born calf that stood shakily before them on four legs.

"It's one of those Siamese," Graham said. Enid had never heard of a Siamese calf before, but there were few words that could describe it better. It was as normal a calf as had ever been born— thin body, shaky legs—except instead of one head, there were two, living off the same frail body. The right head was darker in color and bigger but otherwise each seemed the mirror image of the other. When Graham reached out to pet it, both heads cried out in unison. The calf backed into the corner of the stall and blinked. A little girl, Enid thought, looking at the udders.

"I can't believe it myself," Graham said. Enid moved closer, until she could feel him next to her, solid. Graham put his arm around her, drew her flush against him. She could feel his dry breath against her ear. "Isn't it beautiful?" he said. For the first time in a very long time she felt comfortable in the bend of his arm. She imagined the land changing around her, the clock ticking backwards, the children growing younger until there were none, just her and Graham together.

The calf cried out again. "Hungry," Enid said.

"Yeah, I guess so."

"Where's the happy mother?"

Squeezing Enid tighter, Graham nodded in the direction of the stall next to them. The stall was dark and very quiet. Enid moved to look. Graham shook his head, "It died mid-birth."

One of the farm dogs, the coonhound, crawled from under the fence stall, the white fur about its nose tinged with a deep red, dragging the afterbirth. Enid turned her face into Graham's chest, as he pulled away from her, running the dog off with a pitchfork.

When he returned, Graham walked her back to the house, stood by the bed as she lay down to sleep, telling her he'd be back just as soon as he fed the new calf. When he turned to go, she wondered—as she always seemed to in moments of joy—if things could be like they were in the beginning when she and Graham were first married, when she had felt not so alone.

Enid settled into the comfort of the pillow and heard Graham whistling, so late in the night, as he walked back to the barn. "Everything's Coming Up Roses" drifted through the black air, fluttering almost like a bat who had lost all direction and was suddenly happy to find it again.

In the morning Enid rushed to keep up with breakfast pancakes for the unexpected guests: Doctor Harry, who served as town veterinarian and game warden, and the few eager children from the neighboring farms. She didn't at all mind being the farmer's wife this morning; she could feel Graham's excitement. She looked at him, the boy that sparkled from his wide man's face, and saw vestiges of the person she had married. This day, she couldn't even mind the sweat that bubbled on her forehead and dripped down the side of her face leaving sticky salt trails.

Doctor Harry was the first person Graham had called with the news. When he saw the calf, even he had said that it was a miracle, that he had never seen anything in all his life so extraordinary.

Graham took a bite of pancake. Enid was watching him chew when he looked up at her, and then turned to Doctor Harry, smiling. "We have ourselves a winner. Me and Enid," he said.

Doctor Harry nodded. He had a large, full mustache and a hairline that had receded into the shape of a frying pan on the top of his head. There was a softness about him, though, that Enid could not help but compare any time he and Graham were side by side. It was what had drawn her to him initially when Graham began to worry more about corn and cattle than his own family.

After breakfast, the dishes sitting in the sink, Enid followed everyone to the barn, still in her housecoat. Doctor Harry said they'd be winners for sure, for sure the "People's Choice" at the Mid-Central Pennsylvania Fair in less than one week. Graham knew it. Enid knew it, too. After years of Graham's non-stop obsession with the farm and the fair, the stroke of good fortune had come almost by accident. He'd been trying to win something for years, spending hours alone perfecting methods of breeding and gene-crossing while Enid waited silently by. Of all the categories, the People's Choice was one of the most prestigious. Enid knew that once everyone saw the new calf, they'd surely vote for it. Neither she nor Graham expected to be winning the "Best of Show," but that would have meant selling off the calf to the downtown butcher. People didn't believe in two-headed things anyway, let alone want to eat them.

"So you think we might win something this year," Enid said, smiling from the corner of her mouth. She wanted to hear Doctor Harry's slow soft words, his reassurance, and she did.

As she, Graham, and Doctor Harry neared the barn, the calf was crying: two cries—one high, one low. Graham led the way with the doctor by his side. The calf bleated again. Graham quickened his pace slightly, Enid noticed, knowing he didn't want to appear concerned. She quickened her own to make it seem Graham was not going that fast at all, though the doctor had to step twice to keep up with them.

The children had cornered the calf in the back of the stall, and John Henry, the oldest of their three children at ten and a half, was holding the calf so the others could touch it. "Be careful," he said. "It's fragile." Norma Jean and Carter, her other children, were there, too. The little strawberry-haired girl, Karl Olson's daughter, reached out to pet the smaller of the calf's two heads. "Be careful. I don't know when, but it could split in two anytime." This made the children stand back, especially the Olson girl who jerked her hand and retreated to the outside of the stall.

Graham pushed into the stall, yanked John Henry by the arm, and brained him with the back of his hand. He didn't have to yell for the children to clear out of the stall.

"Stay out of there from now on," Enid said. Doctor Harry grinned at her nervously while the children were scolded. When the children had gone, he told Enid and Graham once again what a prize they had. He and his wife had never had such good fortune, he told them.

Doctor Harry asked if he could take one more look at the calf, although he had already examined it thoroughly before breakfast. Graham nodded and watched him with the careful eye of a parent. Doctor Harry moved his hand over and about the calf. "Amazing how the two heads live off a single heart, just one set of lungs. Must be very stressing on the organs." The heads cried out in unison under his touch.

"Maybe you better let it rest," Graham said. "It's had enough excitement for one morning." He took Doctor Harry lightly by the shoulder and led him out of the barn. "You can see it just like all the paying customers at the fair next week," Graham laughed.

Ralf Wheeley came for Number Nine later that day. Enid and Graham had been cleaning out the old barn when he came driving down the lane, his truck kicking dust behind him.

"What's he doing here?" Enid asked. Graham waved to him and Ralf brought the truck down beside the barn.

"He's come to help with Number Nine." Ralf, only twenty-two, was always eager to help, especially if it involved something tragic or the chance he might impress a woman. He leapt down from the truck and sauntered into the barn, rubbing a fingerful of chew between his lip and gums. He and Graham shook hands. He lowered his chin at Enid; she smiled.

"We gonna load her up?" Ralf said.

"Sure. Enid, maybe you better go to the house."

Enid looked down at the ground, then turned toward the back stall. "I'll just hang around here with our new baby." She tried to smile, but as Ralf opened the gate to where Number Nine lay, a swarm of flies buzzing over the body, she couldn't. Enid tried to entertain herself with the new calf. She talked to it in the cooing voice in which she had spoken to her own children.

Out of the corner of her eye she watched Ralf create a makeshift incline from the ground onto the back of his pick-up with three two-by-fours. Graham was tying the ends of some ropes around Number Nine, around her front legs and midsection.

"Pretty baby . . . pretty babies," Enid said. They hadn't yet decided whether to refer to the calf as one or two.

Ralf started the winch he kept on the back of his pick-up, seemingly for this occasion. Ordinarily he used it to drag brush and firewood down from Winecker's Hollow, often without the Wineckers knowing; sometimes he entered in the tractor pull at the fair. He started the winch. It screeched.

The dead cow budged a little, jerked, and moved toward the back of the truck. The calf started crying. Enid looked at it, looked back at Number Nine. Enid thought of the calf, what it would be like growing up without a mother. She remembered her own father's funeral when she was seventeen. Her father had been a man so consumed by working the land that even at peace his face still seemed to wear the dirt and anguish of everyday toil, the years of smoking. Her mother—a weak woman Enid always thought in some ways too much like herself—did not fare well on her own, becoming less and less of a mother as the years passed, as if Enid had suddenly lost both parents at once.

Graham steadied the cow as it was pulled up the planks and onto the bed of the pick-up. When Ralf cut the power, Number Nine, with her head hanging over the back end, looked out into the barn one last time, her large brown eyes glassy and still. Graham tried to push the cow's head onto the bed so he could shut the tailgate. "Nothing doing. Death's set in hard." He wiped his brow.

Ralf patted Graham on the back, the two shook hands and Ralf jumped into the cab. Then off he went with Number Nine tied down in the back of his truck.

"What's he gonna do with her?" Enid asked.

Graham put his arm around her. "Said he'd cut her up and could sell some parts for half . . . we could use the money."

Enid took a deep breath and held it until the truck and its cloud of dust disappeared, one trailing the other.

Norma Jean had messed her front after riding the Tilt-A-Whirl. John Henry and Carter stood eating blue cotton fluff while Enid wiped the front of her daughter with a moist towelette she had stowed in the small compartment of her purse. Norma Jean stood pulling pieces of cotton candy from Carter who had turned around to stare at the Ferris wheel.

Enid could still not believe this. She and Graham had spent the last few days in anticipation, settling the calf in the livestock area among the other entries, making the proper arrangements, mixing special feed and babying the little calf more than their own children. They had done it all with the simple togetherness of the early years. He allowed her to share in his excitement instead of watching from isolation. Although they had hauled their tomatoes, some corn, and a few of the other cattle off to the fair, it was the calf they were counting on. The final judging was to be on Friday, the last day of the eight-day fair; four days away.

Enid herded the children to the exposition area—the children all the time grabbing at pinwheels and streamers though they had already bought a leash that gave the illusion of an invisible dog, two capguns for each of the boys, and an arm's length of plastic gem bracelets for Norma Jean. People milled about, especially around the stall where Graham was sitting on the edge of the fence. Inside the stall, the calf lay. People walked by and stopped in wonder. Sometimes they would circle back to get a second look. Parents directed their children who would run up to the fence and peer inside. The children seemed most accepting, Enid thought. One woman with a flowered hat made a disgusted face and yanked her little boy by the arm.

Doctor Harry was there, too, talking to Graham and another man Enid did not recognize.

"I'd be willing to buy that little cow from you," the other man said. He had on a T-shirt that was soaked under the arms and that was too small, exposing his round stomach.

"No, she's not for sale," Graham said. Doctor Harry nodded in agreement.

"You don't understand. I'd be willing to pay to make it part of my show."

"Nothing doing." The children started playing hide-and-seek in and around the other stalls. Enid watched Graham look at them and then accusingly at her. She ran after them, grabbing Carter by the arm, telling him to sit. The other ones ran and hid. "Come here, come back," she cried.

"She isn't for sale," Graham said again.

Enid was sure the children had crawled under something. "Norma Jean, John Henry, you come out."

She heard giggling from behind two oil drums. There they were, scrunched up in a pile of manure and straw. They waved to her and started to laugh.

Leading them back to stall fourteen where the entry had been slotted, she could smell their clothing.

Graham was shaking his head.

"Glad to see you didn't sell out to HIM," Doctor Harry declared.

Graham didn't say anything. Norma Jean climbed over the fence, kicking the doctor in the stomach. The calf was no longer afraid of the family. Norma Jean petted both of the heads at the same time. "The other one gets lonely when it doesn't get attention," she said.

"You know, I'd be willing to take that calf off your hands myself," said Doctor Harry. Enid noticed that he had sweatstains under his arms, too.

"What are you going to do with a calf? You barely have room for a yard," Graham smiled and shook his head.

"I'd know as good as anyone how to care for it."

"You don't have a barn, no place for it to run."

"I'd be willing to clean out my woodshed, make it up really nice."

"What would you do with a calf?"

"I'd even be willing to overlook if you take in a few more buck than you should this hunting season," Doctor Harry joked.

Graham put his arm around him and squeezed his thin shoulders. "What you'd do." Doctor Harry became red-faced. Enid climbed over the fence, careful not to let herself kick Doctor Harry though he backed off anyway. She looked at him on the other side of the fence. Enid knew Graham wouldn't sell, and she was happy with that, though she could not help feeling something for Harry.

"She's going to win for sure," Enid said, kneeling beside her daughter. "We're lucky this year. Going to the State Fair. Who knows, maybe this little calf'll carry us all far away from Sinking Springs."

When Enid petted one of the calves' heads, she noticed something had changed. Though it was not particularly noticeable, a thin white film had developed in the corner of one of the eyes. She pointed it out to Graham, but he wasn't particularly worried. "Newborns have lots of little quirks to them," he said. Doctor Harry offered to look, but Graham thanked him and held him by the shoulder. "It'll heal itself. I'm sure there's no cause for alarm."

The white film on the calf's eye did not go away over the next couple of days as Graham had said. The fur around the head became matted down. The calf became sluggish. Each day Enid watched Graham inspect the calf with his wide hands, and each day he nodded his head and said that it seemed to be getting better. Enid knew it wasn't going to get any better, so she turned to Doctor Harry. Whenever there were sick animals on the farm, and because Graham usually believed the sick would heal themselves, Enid was the one to visit Doctor Harry's office several times a year, sometimes without Graham knowing. It was because of Graham's stubbornness that they first began meeting and became friends.

She called Doctor Harry from the pay phone by the grandstand restrooms, and he told her to come right over. Enid left the children with Graham, telling him she'd buy some baked goods and produce in the meantime, to which Graham nodded and gathered the children around him. Enid knew he was reluctant to leave the calf unattended, especially since the calf was getting sicker. The last sound Enid heard as she walked away was the voice of Norma Jean begging for a snow-cone.

Doctor Harry's office was a red brick building that had once been a house and was set at the end of a long line of trees. No one was in the waiting room, and the part-time receptionist showed Enid into one of Doctor Harry's two offices. A long, metal table was in the center of the room with a large light suspended above it, hanging down from the ceiling. Beyond the examining table was a wooden desk and chair and a makeshift bookshelf that in some places was oddly angled, giving the impression of poor workmanship. The most striking things about the office, however, were the stuffed heads of various sorts along the walls; all were living animals once. "Taxidermy's a little hobby of mine," Doctor Harry had said the first time she had come to him eight or nine years ago. Enid looked at each one of the trophies every time she entered. A twelve-point buck, a ram's head, a rainbow-scaled marlin, a pheasant posed as if caught in midflight. "This one's from New Mexico. This one I wrangled in Saskatchewan," he had told her. For Enid, their rigid frozenness, as if time had stopped for them, made her uncomfortable. She couldn't help feeling like she was the one that was going to be examined.

Enid picked up a copy of *Field & Stream*, began paging through, looking at the pictures. Sometimes she would compare the sketches of deer and fish in the *Field & Stream* to the trophies that hung along the walls. She heard the doorknob begin to turn and closed the magazine. Doctor Harry entered smiling.

"Call me a straight-out liar," he said.

"What?"

"A straight-out liar. How many years have I been telling you now that I'd subscribe to something for my female customers to read?"

"About as long as I've been coming to you."

"Hopefully next time I see you, you'll be in for a surprise. What do you like? *Redbook? Better Homes & Gardens?*" Doctor Harry lifted himself onto the examining table with his hands and sat there, his legs dangling down. "So how can I help you?" Enid looked at him and remembered the times she had wondered how her life would have been different if she had married Doctor Harry. There used to be times, even, when she felt that if Doctor Harry had wanted to kiss her, she would have let him. But he had never pressed that far.

"It's the calf," she finally said.

"Ah, and here I thought you came to see me. I should have known better."

"It doesn't seem to be getting any better, and you know how stubborn Graham can be about getting help."

Doctor Harry nodded. "So what would you like me to do?"

"What do you think's wrong with it? Is there anything I could—"

Doctor Harry's face wrinkled. He put his hand against his mouth and shifted his eyes toward the ceiling. "You could just sell it to me, and it'd be off your hands completely."

"I don't think Graham would want to—"

"Here. Let me show you something." Doctor Harry pushed himself off the table and went over the bookshelf. He pulled a large, thick photo album from the top and sat down next to Enid on the green vinyl sofa. "My wife and I, we go a lot of places, together. I told you all the stories. Anyway, you know one of our favorite places is Paris." Enid recalled the many times she had visited with Doctor Harry and how he talked often about his wife, their travels, their problems. This had spurred Enid to entrust him with her own feelings when Graham ignored her and grew cold. She remembered Doctor Harry's story of Paris most of all and how she had thought of visiting there after her father had given her the encyclopedia set when she was twelve years old. "It was the most beautiful thing," Doctor Harry continued. "My wife and I drank wine in the open-air cafés along the Boulevard St.-Germain, close to the famous Notre Dame cathedral." Enid looked intently at the photographs, how they had captured the place so clearly and contained it within the square of the film paper. Even Doctor Harry's smiling wife was a captive of sorts. Doctor Harry described to Enid the famous rose window and how if the sun caught it just right the whole church was lit up with the prettiest light one could ever see. Enid imagined herself there, caught and suspended in that light. These pictures were far more alive, Enid thought, than those she and Graham had ever posed for in their backyard or during their one trip to the national park.

"Here's my wife. Here were are in front of the Eiffel Tower."

Enid felt herself being drawn in, more and more.

"My wife just adores crepes." Enid looked at a picture of Doctor Harry's wife holding a fork to her mouth and pretending to take a bite. She stared at it for a few moments before she realized that Doctor Harry had stopped talking and was looking directly at her.

"You know Graham and I go way back, but I feel I just have to say this, Enid. He's not treating you like he should. In fact, I don't think he realizes what a great woman he's got."

Enid stared down at the photographs. "Doctor Harry—" She knew things could get better between her and Graham now. He had already shown a change.

"I'm just saying that I could give you the money you need. Don't think that I don't remember the times you've told me how much you've wanted from your life. And what you're doing to the calf is a waste. A thing like you and Graham have should be preserved—"

"Really, I just came to see if you knew of any medication—"

"Well, I'll tell you what," Doctor Harry said as he closed the album. "Why don't I drop by the fairgrounds later tonight, and I'll have a look at the calf?"

"Can't you just—"

"I really need to look at it before I can prescribe any medication."

Enid looked at the floor. She felt Doctor Harry's hand come to rest and steady on her shoulder. This wasn't what she wanted. "What time? I don't know . . . I mean Graham and I'll probably leave after eight or so."

"Good, that's good. I'll stop by the fairgrounds around eleven. Meet me there, right?"

"But I don't see what for, and what will I tell—"

"Tell Graham you forgot something. Tell him you need to blow off some steam, whatever gets you out of the house. . . ."

Enid shook her head. "I don't know . . . what about you?"

"It'll be all right. I'll make up something for my wife. Come on, Enid, we're old friends."

She picked up her purse and thought about the calf becoming even sicker as they spoke. "Thank you," she said.

"And think about what I said. Imagine what you two could do with that extra money. You and Graham could even go to Paris. It's like you've always wanted."

Enid and Graham sat at the wooden picnic table after spending an hour playing bingo-ball with the children. She was sure their chances of winning had been slim, but somehow they came out of the whole venture with a plastic alarm clock and three posters. It had only cost them ten dollars. Graham was eating his second sloppy-joe. Enid sensed a change in him, felt almost as if he were looking right through her. She watched him chew; sometimes the orange-red meat stuck from the corner of his mouth until he pulled it in with his tongue.

Enid found herself looking at her watch, wondering when they would leave so she could eventually come back and meet Doctor Harry. It was still hours away.

She heard the sound of organ music grow louder around the corner of the food trailer. A man in a red costume with gold-plaited trim churned the crank of a hand organ. With a bushy black beard, the organ grinder looked a lot like the spider monkey that was perched on his shoulder and dressed in duplicate. The monkey leapt back and forth between the ground and the man's shoulder, running up to people with its tin cup and tipping its hat when they gave him a coin. Enid watched the man direct the monkey with a tug of the leash that collared its furry neck. The three children jumped up from the table and went running. The monkey sprang to the safety of the bearded man's shoulder. Enid started to laugh and urged Graham to turn around and see. "Look, Graham." He didn't turn around. "Look." When he didn't move, she knew something was the matter.

"So you think we should sell it?" Graham's low voice slid among the bright sounds of the organ grinder and the bumper cars, the laughing children, the calliope.

Enid faced him over the table. "What are you talking about?"

"I think you know. I've been thinking maybe we should sell that calf. Either to Doctor Harry or that other guy, but I guess we should sell it to the Doc. He's been a friend all these years. He's offered twenty-five hundred dollars for it."

"Twenty-five hundred dollars?" Enid thought of all the possibilities. "But you wanted to win and go on to the State Fair. What changed?"

"Just a feeling."

Enid started to clear away the trash from the table. She crumbled the napkins and paper cups and dropped them into the blue oil-drum garbage can. "Must be more than just a feeling. Of all the years I've known you, I don't remember one time when you acted on a feeling."

The melody of the hand organ bled into the conversation.

"Doctor Harry told me what you said, Enid. About me, about what you want."

Enid turned around slowly. She felt the tension pull along the length of her neck, a hot-cold feeling rush into her face. "What are you talking about?"

"Doctor Harry told me how he's been keeping it all a secret to protect me and how you've been telling *him* for years."

Enid looked at the ground. "Graham, that's not true . . . not all true."

"You don't have to say anything. I know what I know. That's why I think we should just off and sell it right after the judging tomorrow, whether we'd go on to the state level or not."

"But what about going on to the state fair. That's what we really wanted—"

"My word's the last word. I'm not talking about it anymore."

Enid sat down at the picnic table with her back to Graham and stared blankly at the children and the monkey man. With each tug of the leash, he brought the monkey right back to where he wanted him.

Many times before they left the fairgrounds, Enid tried to make Graham believe her, but he had already made up his mind. She felt further from him than ever before, as they walked around the fair silently and stood watch over the calf. Several times she had to turn away and hide her face in her hands just in case she would start to cry.

The ride home that night was not filled with the children's laughter. More than anything, Enid wanted Graham to take her in his arms and smooth her hair, so she would know that she wasn't alone, that she had not pushed him away when they were coming close again.

The sunlight slipped from the sky, and Enid thought of returning to the fairgrounds later that night, wondered what would happen. She wondered if she could even stand to face Doctor Harry. She would want to yell at him and tell him, "No," that the calf wasn't for sale. Once home, she spent the time looking out through the kitchen window at the barn. Graham stared at the television with a silence that enraged her.

At exactly 10:20, Enid announced she was going for a drive. She fumbled for her own words but found instead Doctor Harry's: "I need to blow off some steam."

The children had brushed their teeth for bed and were sleeping when she took the car keys from the hook in the kitchen. Graham didn't turn around to look at her. "You know where I'll be," he said, each word slipping slowly, one after the other, from his lips.

Enid stopped for a moment by the door, waiting for the chill to pass through her, but it didn't completely. It stayed with her as she stepped into the yard and went to the car that sat under the clean view of moonlight. Enid could not keep her mind on the road. She kept thinking of what Graham had said, and the more she thought about it, the more she convinced herself of the subtle sarcasm concealed among his words. When she arrived at the fairgrounds minutes later, she had no idea how she had gotten there and remembered nothing of the drive.

Many of the people were starting to leave, and the lights were beginning to dim for the evening. The stalls were left in almost darkness, except for a few incandescent bulbs that glowed like fireflies throughout the area at designated points. She heard some of the livestock shuffling from slumber at her presence.

The calf was sleeping when she came to stall fourteen. It was breathing heavily, and in the shadows, it looked worse than it had earlier in the day. Enid called to it. Its eyes blinked open, and it pushed itself up on its wobbly legs. Enid saw the one eye had gone almost completely white. The fur on both heads was wet and matted together, covered with dried mucus around the mouth and nose. She touched the calf's head, felt its dirty, thick fur against the softness of her fingers. She knew Doctor Harry would be coming soon.

Enid looked at the calf doing its best to stay standing and keep its head under her twirling fingers. She could hear its troubled breath passing back and forth through its airways. The calf nudged her hand when she stopped scratching. She looked again at the calf's white eye, almost completely full as a moon in phase. It had begun to look like the unreal eyes of Doctor Harry's trophies. She pictured him plucking out the calf's eyes and putting glass marbles in their place. Then she imagined the calf posed and standing in the office around the galvanized examining table. Each time one of the farm animals would get sick, she would be the one to come face to face with the calf and each time be reminded of how she had hurt Graham. Even if she and Graham would travel, even if he would forgive her in time, she would have to remember this day, always come back to this time, remembering Graham staring silently at the TV while she tried to imagine his thoughts.

She undid the lock and latch and opened the gate to the stall. The calf wobbled slowly forward, pressing one of its heads through the opening. It was the one with the white eye. She pushed the gate farther open and watched the calf stagger out beside her. She turned away, not wanting to see it struggle so with walking. It was dirty, almost loathsome.

"Go," Enid said. The calf stood silently beside her. "Go," but the calf didn't move. She nudged it in the side, then kicked it when it didn't go. The calf staggered from her to the end of the row of stalls some thirty feet away. Before it could return, Enid broke into a run and ran all the way back to the car, not stopping until she was safely inside. One after the other, the colored lights started to blink out all over the fairgrounds, and the carnival rides ceased to move. Enid breathed in, put the key in the ignition, and drove off just minutes before she was to meet with Doctor Harry.

When Graham wrestled her from sleep the next morning, Enid lay still for a moment and remembered a dream. She had been aboard a large, drifting ship, empty, with ripped, flowing sails that blew snakelike in the wind. Graham was there and her parents, too, all in the same drifting ship. She had turned into the sun just long enough that when she looked back again, they were all gone, except for watery footprints where they had stood before, as if they had melted in the time it took her to look away. She heard the sound, the low mournful baying coming from below. With salt mist dried and stuck to her face, she peered over the edge as the sound came again. She saw her face, her reflection that wriggled and lost shape each time a wave passed nearby. A hand reached out of the water, toward her neck, and she broke through the thin wall of sleep to feel Graham's large hand on her shoulder. He didn't say anything, but went about getting ready for the morning.

The children were more excited than usual, hitting each other with spoons at breakfast and choking each other with seatbelts once they had all piled into the car. Graham was silent the whole way to the fair, just as he had greeted her in bed when she returned the night before.

After Graham parked the truck, Enid and the children followed him single file to the livestock area. Enid felt the strange presence of her heart in her chest. When they came in view of the empty stall, Graham stopped short and let out a sharp gasp. He ran forward, leaned over the gate, then started looking into the surrounding stalls with frantic energy. "It's gone."

The children ran beside their father, and Enid pretended to search for the missing calf.

Graham ran up and down the aisles checking each stall. Enid noticed three white-haired men with clipboards making their way into the livestock area. She knew they were the judges. Graham ran up to them. The one had colored ribbons overflowing from his side pocket. "I lost my calf. It's gone."

"It's been kidnapped," yelled John Henry.

"I bet the monkey-man took it," chimed Carter.

The judges started speaking to Graham, but Enid couldn't hear what they were saying from where she stood.

"I'm going to the fair security," Graham said, brushing past Enid and the children. The judges continued with their clipboards.

When Graham returned a few minutes later, his face was wet with sweat and red.

"They didn't find it yet, but they will."

Enid began to wonder. Graham paced back and forth. Enid instructed the children to sit quietly. They finally settled in the corner of the stall where the calf had lain.

Enid was sitting with her face in her hands when she heard footsteps behind her. She looked up. It was Doctor Harry. "What's happened?" She knew the question asked for more than she could tell. He put his hand on her shoulder and rubbed into her back with his thumb.

"It's gone," Graham said.

Doctor Harry's face wrinkled up. He removed his hand from Enid's shoulder.

They waited until a blond teenage boy came running back through the stalls. "We found it, sir," he said to Graham. The children got up from the straw. "They should probably stay here."

Enid knew it was dead, even before she saw it, and she told the children to stay just where they were until she came back. She went with Graham, and Doctor Harry followed close behind them. Enid pressed her shoulder tight against Graham's, so that Doctor Harry's attempts at conversation went almost unheard.

The boy led them to the base of the Ferris wheel where high weeds grew around dark and green. He stomped the front weeds down with his booted foot to reveal a thin, blue-wool blanket laid over a small heap. "It's dead," the boy said. "Looks like something tore at it, around the gut." The boy lifted the cover, but Enid didn't look. Instead she looked up at the spinning Ferris wheel and thought of the first time she rode it years ago when her parents had strapped her into the seat and sent her spinning toward the top. Each time she had come close to the ground, she could see her mother and father, her mother in polished whiteness and her father with an odd panama hat. She wanted off but was swept up again and again while they waved at her and grinned. Then it stopped. She was held at the top, calling to her parents who looked like all the other people on the ground from up so high. The solitary stillness made her cry. It was only years later with Graham that she had had the courage to ride the Ferris wheel a second time. She remembered how he had held her and made her laugh as they wheeled around and around.

"We need to take it home and bury it," Enid said. Doctor Harry turned sharply and looked at her. She could read the disappointment and anger in his face. Then she turned and looked at Graham. His eyes seemed set back further in his head, his cheeks hung soft and tensionless.

She felt his body begin to shudder beside her. He spoke slowly. "I'm sorry, Enid. I know how you—"

"I'm going to get the kids." She couldn't let him finish. She ran her fingers across the back of his head and through his hair. "I'll meet you at the truck. I'm sure Doctor Harry will help you carry the calf."

She squeezed Graham's hand and turned to go. The fair was all around.

When she entered the exposition area, the livestock stalls were being decorated with multicolored prize ribbons, all flapping in the wind. She looked at them—red, yellow, and blue—like miniature sails. The children came clambering out of the stall toward her when she called for them.

It was a difficult thing to say, but she told the children the truth. She took Norma Jean, who had started to sniffle tears, by the hand. The boys came after them. Enid looked at all the colors surrounding her and her children, looked at the live-eyed animals that peered up from their stalls not understanding. As she and her children passed the last stall, Enid stopped to look.

Inside was a strong black calf, thick in the middle, with sinewy legs. It stared at her as she examined the ribbon posted beside its stall. It was the flowery kind with the big button center and cloth ruffled all around. Enid mouthed the words in gold lettering: First Place, People's Choice.

She heard the life of the fair all about her, children screaming inside glass-mirrored houses and honking bumper cars. She knew the carrousel animals were chasing each other in circles and there were funnel cakes and french fries and good things. She pulled her children close and looked back at the winning calf's stall. As if keeping time, the blue ribbon flapped in the wind.

the clay is vile

I f once, a thousand times. John quickens passing that eyesore. He's not afraid, not particularly afraid, yet the sight of the house speeds his heart, makes him think of the house, the burden of it, nothing but. History, warred and yet unsettled, speaks everywhere, from the horribly orange tin roof to the windows marred by spider-cracks to the small balcony threatening to free itself from the second story, taking out anything, anyone gawking, lingering below. A doorless white refrigerator rules the front porch. Cats, black and gray and bluish black, swirl from the refrigerator's rusted shelves, swatting flies, biting tails, and stare toward the road as if expecting someone—anyone!—who might mix up their time.

Someone must live in the house. What to make of the Victory Garden in the front yard? Normal people would condemn such a thing to the back of their properties, the unsightly tangle of binder-twine and posted seed-packets proclaiming tomatoes "tomatoes" hidden from view. John recognizes pepper plants, stalks of sweet corn at least two feet in height. Aluminum pie plates clatter, strung up to discourage birds.

Maybe it's because he runs so early that he doesn't see anyone here, that there's no one, ever, to connect to this house. Of course there are stories, wisps of tales relating madness and hard luck. Due to the house's desperate state, due to its current look of abuse and misuse, it can be nothing else but haunted. For most people, the house is fortunately far enough from town, a horrible thought that's only entertained in passing, a wrong turn down the wrong road. No car or truck or motorcycle has ever taken up the space of the driveway as far as John knows. There are no comings and goings, other than sighs that come directly from the house. John hears them: old air caught and sweeping through rooms. He imagines ghosts on top of ghosts, packed and compressed until all individual spirits have given way to, combine to form, one large powerful mass.

Always he turns to watch the house disappear behind him as he runs. He's not sure why. Maybe because he needs to know it's gone. Each and every morning as he rounds the turn of the road, the house blinks, then cedes completely to trees and fog, and then, always, John slows to the normal cadence of his five-mile run. The blonde hairs on his arm glisten with sweat and dew. He thinks then of Nathan, still sleeping, how he will wake Nathan with force once home, how Nathan will murmur and whimper lost in the last dream of morning, before John and Nathan will kiss and roll together in that first part of their day together that isn't sleep.

So often John is the first to slide from the sheets after sex, leaving Nathan to linger among the intimacy of pillows. In the bathroom, John switches on the radio, the same morning station, and studies himself in the mirror to be sure nothing has changed—no crow's feet, no timelines creasing his forehead. Then he shaves, always pleased to see how young he can look, not a day over twenty-five, a ripe age. Nathan's only twenty, a kid, the way John likes, preferring to be the stronger, in control of the relationship, thus having the option—should it ever arise—of using force to end arguments, decide decisions, have his own way. He, like Nathan, has lived in the small town of Sinking Springs, Pennsylvania, all his life, except for the brief stint at the state college, satellite campus, needing only a month to realize what he's looking for couldn't be found in books. He and Nathan met by mistake in the aisle of the SuperFresh—what's said about supermarkets is true!—and they've been living together for six months. "To save money," John says. "What we have can end at any time. We're not married. Certainly not."

John fears he's the less smart of the pair. Nathan reads and reads, clutters their small, usually neat house with novels and scraps of paper scribbled with interesting quotes. Sometimes, drinking prune juice for his slow digestion, Nathan talks of going to school. "Maybe an education is just the thing I need."

"You should be happy with your job at the bank," John tells him. "You should be happy here with me."

Nathan nods, cries some for thinking so selfishly. John leaves the room—to cut an apple into fours, pay the phone bill, polish shoes—giving Nathan the time to fill himself with bad-feeling.

On occasion John and Nathan drive to Baltimore or Philadelphia or down to D.C. to stop at all-men bars, once—against better judgment—a dance club. How odd to see men dancing: it was not right, John thought, one man holding another's arms the way a woman might, so publicly displayed. Freedom should have limits. Nathan swayed along the wall, bobbing his head. John made him stop. Later that night shirts were pulled over heads, the bare-chested revelers sweaty and now so free. For a moment the snap-tight resistance in John slackened. Had Nathan been home and sleeping, had a tank of a man not stumbled into them, looking them up and down and up, saying, "Come on, guys," grabbing Nathan's hem: only then might John's resistance more noticeably acquiesced.

"That's another kind of life," said John. "A life we won't be part of. They're sick, embarrassing the way they live so fast and easy."

"Don't worry," Nathan said, "I like to know the person I'm sleeping with."

When Nathan says such stupid things, John feels disgusted, less human, as if some awful protuberance has matured inside him, a parasite that is like guilt but not. Guilt would make him stop, make him change his ways, but this thing—that is like guilt but not—lacks all feeling of *regret.* John keeps his infidelities a secret, the few guys he's met and fucked at deserted rest stops along the turnpike, men he's discovered in chat rooms of America Online—the one computer skill he felt compelled to learn. He's left work early some days to meet these men, to drive to Gettysburg or Pageant or Alta Ridge, making up lies when Nathan asks why John's paycheck is smaller than usual. "Taxes," John says. "Something with taxes." Any further explanation—to Nathan, to himself, to anyone—would require more soul-searching, a greater commitment to self-evaluation than John is ready to make.

Weekday mornings, after dropping Nathan at the bank, John drives through town passing the SuperFresh, the Mobil station on the far side of town. He passes the newly opened Borders Bookstore where the other six faggots of Sinking Springs spend

Friday nights dreaming after high school boys. Eventually these
odd fat men with sideburns and mustaches pair up, one fat old
man fucking another, or the old faggots go home singly, alone, to
the less complicated love of soft-cover porn. Sitting together in
the seldom crowded bookstore cafe, John and Nathan laugh at
these old men, their leering and their gawking; for John and
Nathan a certain happiness lies in having one another, the security of comfort, of not having to find someone with whom to
share sleep.

The Wal-Mart where John works is in Tysonville, a thirty-
minute drive. His job in the film processing department pays well
enough, allows him to work alone or with only one person, usually Shirley, an abandoned wife with two kids, who eats carrot
sticks for lunch and ginger snaps at breaks. She reads self-help
books, is nice to talk to, and harmless. She's fanatically religious,
in that she can't get enough of religions, any and all of them. She
goes to church each Sunday morning, Episcopalian, yet she med-
itates, deals Tarot, believes in crystal healing. A pouch of semi-
precious stones dangles from her neck. She knows about voodoo
dolls, visions, mummification. She doesn't know about John and
Nathan, thinks instead they are two very good friends, two good-
looking young men who happen to share rent. Not that Shirley
would be unaccepting, John thinks. Shirley's the pit of accep-
tance, accepting anything that can be cast in some—whether
weak or strong—good light.

John's not much of a photographer, though he enjoys taking
pictures. To get his job, he didn't need to lie as he'd been planning.
This, John thinks, had something to do with looks, the way he
looks, like he could be both photographer and photographee. He
prides himself on his physique, how it went naturally from the
lithe muscles of a mediocre high school basketball forward to the
larger yet more compact scale reached through weights and
presses and push-ups.

The darkroom, developing film, is John's favorite part of the day. He's empowered watching scenes of life color before him, taking shape slowly and steadily in the developing pan or zipping through photo-processing. He and those who work different shifts in the film department post copies of all nude photos onto a wall, concealed from store management by a large glossy calendar from the local Chinese restaurant, Kung Bo Express. The Wall of Shame. The wall's largely covered, taken over by breasts and vaginas and cocks. In one photo, an old man in a wheelchair stretches his limp and uncircumcised penis toward his belly button. In another, a mousy woman in a waitress hat, a woman John's seen before at the Tysonville Family Restaurant, shoves her tits into another woman's mouth. There are pictures of children, naked, disturbing in their young nudity, the burden of sexuality forced upon them. Some pictures show bruises, messed hair, worse. When John or one of the other developers spy such haunting images, they're sure to write PD on the film pack, just so whoever happens to be working when the pedophile comes to pick up the photos can stare *you're sick* into the man or woman's face. These horrible people are not always the one's you'd expect. They are not always the ugly, the weak, the undesired.

John's made copies only of the adult photos, also the ones of boys who look eighteen. He keeps them in a travel pamphlet for the Poconos, tucked inside the deep pocket of a sports coat at the back of the bedroom closet, the sports coat hidden behind too small winter jackets, a hanger of bad ties. The pictures John takes of him and Nathan naked, of them having sex, he develops himself. He's never been an exhibitionist. Nathan, John thinks, would say the same.

Shirley is the only developer actually known to have reported potential pedophiles as wished by federal law. Too, she's the only one disturbed by the wall of nudity. Such bad vibes. One night she had a dream that the photographs came to life, spoke their

secrets. She turns from the wall whenever she enters the darkroom, won't look at it ever. She has her kids to think of. She lets
John do the developing when he's around, doesn't mind waiting
on customers. John thinks the wall of nudity will never disgust
him. He'll never have kids.

Throughout the summer, the Victory Garden in front of the old
house flourishes. Fat tomatoes split, aching to be plucked from
their vines. The corn sprouts tassels, stalks are engorged with ears.
Even so early in the morning, fly-swarms hover over the garden
and whirl like thoughts trying to find shape.

The morning John decides to pick the vegetables, he straps
his old college knapsack to his broad back. It feels strange,
reminds him of the horrible experience of higher education, how
for a month he'd filled the knapsack—just like the other students
had—with hefty texts and ripped papers and spiral notebooks
whose wire binding always seemed to unravel, jabbing him,
breaking his skin every time he reached into the bag. He recalls
sitting in chemistry class, twirling pencils through his fingers, listening to a small man talk about dissociated ions, covalent bonds,
words without purpose.

The house appears, as it always does, shifting shape through
the trees until it comes in full view. The orange roof, the cinderblock chips forming a garden walk, the twisted weather vane
that points nowhere but WEST, the way John's come—these
things greet him. The action of stopping is surprisingly easy.
From the road, John watches the house, as if waiting for it to
make the first move. Curtains hold their windowframes. A black-
bird rests, then flutters from the roof peak. No one's home.

John strides up the hill, into the yard and garden abuzz with
gnats and gadflies. Though there hasn't been rain for some time,
the earth's soft, wet. Heavy striations of red clay run like arteries

in and among the roots of plants. John's seen this type of clay before, found in much smaller portions along the Susquehanna River, at the bottom of lakes and ponds. He's heard two things. One: that the clay is rich in nutrients. Two: that the clay is not. This clay emits a strange yeasty scent. He's never seen it so thickly concentrated as in the garden.

A horrible mewing as the cats leap from the porch. Urgent, they trot and hop across the yard, poke their heads through the tall yard grass, surround his feet, rubbing their matted and prickly fur against his ankles and bare legs. There must be fifteen or twenty of them, some grossly thin, scabrous around their noses and pink anuses, all of them mewing, wanting attention and to be fed. "Where'd you guys come from?" John asks.

He slips the pack from his shoulders. Holding back leaves, he fills his knapsack with the best tomatoes, pushes away the cats that keep trying to climb inside. He strips ears of corn from their stalks. The cats bite his ankles, follow him, looking at anything he looks at.

The knapsack bulges, is a slight, annoying hump now on his back. He won't call what he's done "stealing." It's "saving," from waste. He bends, one last time, to pick a small cherry tomato, brushing away the red dirt, an unhappy bug. Standing he looks back at the house, bites the tomato from its top and stem. Often he's wondered what the house is like inside. The thought of entering someone's house: possessing it as if it were his own. He's imagined the squalor, rotted and mouse-filled mattresses fermenting on the floor, doll parts, paintings without frames, a fireplace filled with fledgling cranes that've plummeted to their deaths. He imagines that the interior, each and every room, would be cold, even in summer.

The cats follow him to the edge of the yard. One jumps at his leg, draws blood, skitters down, claws digging into his shoe. John shakes the cat off. It blinks, yawns. John starts to run, building speed, thinking he'll get an even better workout this morning with the extra weight strapped to his back.

No bruises, not a one. No bad spots, no worms, no inedible parts.

"Where'd you find this stuff?" Nathan asks. In the pallid light of the kitchen and morning, he's thin, a rail standing in boxer shorts that aren't his size. Filling the sink with water, he crunches and crosses his toes, scratches the side of his smooth leg.

"A secret known only to me," John says.

"Sounds like you."

"What sounds like me?"

"A secret."

Nathan likes to talk of feelings. John doesn't, talking about such things doesn't come naturally, has no utility. Even talking about the weather is preferable. Why talk of something so untouchable, so unpredictable? Talk of the weather prepares you for storms, allows you to grab an umbrella, rain gear. Not so of feelings. Talk of them prepares you for nothing, clouds your mind with worry. Since the beginning of their relationship, Nathan, like so many others who choose imperfect love, assumes feelings don't and can't exist without giving them words.

Nathan takes the sweet white corn, shucks it, frees it from its green casing as if it were something he's born to do. John stands behind him at the sink, wraps his arms across Nathan's soft chest, pinches a nipple. On Nathan's left shoulder is a tattoo, a small pulsing heart pierced through with an arrow. John marvels at how easily he eclipses Nathan. It would take two Nathans to fill the body of one John, almost. He's so small and wonderful in John's arms.

Nathan finishes, is so efficient, presents a bag of corn and tomatoes. "For Shirley. We'll have ours tonight for dinner."

Nathan wipes the kitchen counter, fast broad stripes. "I love you," he says. It comes out sounding like a question. "I'm going to take a shower."

"Uh-huh," John says. He watches Nathan leave, Nathan's small ass. John's horny, would love to have sex again before going to work. Although it won't succeed, he could try climbing into the shower with Nathan. They haven't showered together for a long time, the act of bathing and cleansing has become again private, a reason for embarrassment. John stands at the bathroom door, listening to the humming, Nathan's baritone humming a silly song.

The water keeps coming. John pushes aside the winter coats and the hanger of bad ties at the back of the bedroom closet, finds the old sports blazer, opens the pocket and the travel brochure to the photographs tucked safely inside. He can get himself off in two minutes. It's not as fun, but much less complicated. It ends the same.

Little can be developed. The red light's gone out. Someone forgot to reorder bulbs. Customers complain about their film.

"You said today," an old woman sneers.

"Now I'm saying tomorrow, come back tomorrow."

"But last week, you told me today."

"Come back tomorrow."

When no customers are in eye- or earshot, Shirley opens the leather pouch around her neck, extracts a finger-sized quartz crystal, and waves it over the countertop. "Away bad energy, away." It's a joke, and yet not. Though she's smirking, waiting for John's reaction, somewhere in her heart or her mind, Shirley's thinking she's doing some good.

John lets her to hold down the fort, drives to pick up another bulb. When he returns, Shirley has her crystal arsenal spread in an arc on the counter: several white quartz, rose quartz, amethyst, jade and citrine, uncut peridot. In her right hand she fingers a rosary. "Five more complainers," she says and she's still smiling, can joke about the worst of experiences. "All this negativity comes down to nothing. Certainly not fixing the broken lightbulb."

"How do you do it?" John asks. "You keep so cool."

"My supplies. Get yourself a rock garden, you'll notice changes."

"No really."

"It must be my kids then."

"That's your answer to everything. Kids. There has to be something else."

Shirley collects her stones as if they were brittle eggs. She slides them into the pouch around her neck. "I still say kids. Invest yourself in something, it eats you up. Sometimes people say 'Shirley,' I forget they're talking to me, I'm so used to being 'Mom.'" She thinks a moment more; her fingertip investigates a scab at the corner of her mouth. "Kids, and maybe faith in something better than me. That's my honest answer. And really, aren't they the same?" For a moment John feels there is something so true in the air between him and Shirley that he forces himself to laugh.

In the darkroom, he unscrews the dead lightbulb. It feels explosive, ready to shatter, and cold. "When are you going to introduce me to your girlfriend?" Shirley asks. She swats him on the butt. "If I were younger I'd be chasing that tail."

"You would?"

"You know it. But I'll be happy to be your mama. Call me Mama Shirley." A mother's the last thing John wants, a father too; he would like to tell Shirley she's already more mother and father to him in some ways than his own who live on the other side of Sinking Springs in a once kind white house that's ceased its welcoming of anyone.

"Careful, electrician at work," says John. He screws in the bulb, tries the light. He catches Shirley staring at the Wall of Shame. "See something you like?"

She points, opens her mouth, but doesn't speak.

"It's okay," John says. "There are worse things in the world."

"I thought for a minute there was a picture of me up there," Shirley says.

"Not that I know of. I would've warned you."

"Would you?"

In the middle of the night, past midnight, John wakes to find Nathan running for the bathroom. He hears gagging, the flush of a toilet.

Nathan's bent over, his small thin frame shakes violently, like it's cold, terribly cold, but the house isn't colder than usual. The air conditioning's on, just enough to keep summer out-of-doors.

"Holy shit do I feel sick," Nathan says. His eyes water. He keeps leaning over the toilet to gag. "I feel like it'll come out both ends."

"You gonna be okay?"

"Yeah, go back to bed."

John tries to sleep but can't because of Nathan's constant waking, his restlessness, his running to and from the bathroom. Once, around 2:00 A.M., Nathan doesn't quite make it. What a stench. It finds every place in the house, touches each and every corner. John turns off the air conditioner, throws open the windows. The night's warm and wet, bubbling in at him through the screens.

"I'm sleeping in the living room," John says. "Christ, what did we eat?" He thinks of the corn on the cob, tomato sandwiches slathered with mayonnaise, how he and Nathan sat in the backyard, how Nathan talked on and on about what a perfect evening it was.

"I can't believe you're not sick too," Nathan says.

"Not yet. I have the better constitution." John arranges pillow and blanket on the couch that is lumpy and soft. It seems more inviting in its lack of support than it actually is. The clock on the television ticks loudly. John listens to the gagging, it continues, the upheaval and expulsion of things fouling in Nathan's stomach.

"I feel like I'm going to die," Nathan yells at one point. He yells at himself, at his stomach. "There can't be anything left in there. There can't be anything left."

The drive to work is slow, one John's not made often alone. He listens to the radio, counts the number of cars that pass. These things seem only to make the drive longer.

Shirley's supposed to work, too, but hasn't come in yet. First she's fifteen, thirty, then sixty minutes late. The phone rings.

"I'm not going to make it to work today," she says. "We're all sick. Sick as dogs."

"Must be something going around."

"Must be. The boys are sick in bed. We spent a horrible night."

"Well, take care of yourselves."

"We are. I already have a remedy cooking on the stove. I'll be back tomorrow. Don't worry."

"Why would I worry?"

Nathan's started to wander. When John comes home from work, he finds Nathan sitting beneath a potted fern in the corner of the living room. "It's cold in here," Nathan says. "I was pretending I'm under a palm tree, someplace warmer."

John can't tell if it's delirium or Nathan's being funny. "Did you eat anything today?"

"I drank some water. Good for the system."

"You need to get some food in you."

John throws together a pasty meal, lots of carbohydrates, things that will bind Nathan's stomach: spaghetti, cheese sandwiches, noodles in broth.

"I don't want any of it," he says. "I keep thinking of worms."

"Worms?"

"Worms that are in my skin."

"You should go lie down."

"I'm fine now that I'm moving, now that I'm up and around," Nathan says. "I feel a little better."

"You should lie down."

"I'm not tired."

"Still you should lie down."

During the night, Nathan sleepwalks. John wakens, alone, hearing the noises of Nathan's journey through other rooms. John doesn't switch on lights but watches through the dark as Nathan makes it to the kitchen for a glass of water. Then he slumbers to the bathroom closet, taking down a towel and then another and then dropping them onto the floor. John follows behind, picking them up, returning them to their proper place. At times Nathan seems to be awake, his eyes are glistening and focused on whatever it is he happens to be doing.

"Christ, Nathan, what's going on?" John says. But nothing will wake or stop Nathan. He's moving about the house, through the unlighted and empty rooms, before returning to bed where John wraps his arms about him, tries to hold him still.

Nathan used to sleepwalk as a child. His parents installed a special gate to keep him from plummeting down stairs. John remembers hearing that this sort of thing, walking in one's sleep, stayed with a person, regardless of age.

In the morning, Nathan seems well enough to make love. He wants to anyway, whether he's feeling one hundred percent or not. For the twenty minutes it takes the two of them to start and finish, Nathan is healthy, young, warm, and impassioned, but when it's over, he says he's tired. He falls into sleep.

"You were crazy last night," John says. Nathan doesn't remember a thing. John puts on his running shoes, his shorts, but when he gets to the door, he stops, reconsiders. The lack of sleep, tossing and turning, has turned his legs to stone. No, he won't go running today.

There's nothing left of it. The Wall of Shame is gone. A clean gray wall, that's all that's left, uncovered from behind the photographs. John traces his fingers between the cinderblocks, as if making sure the wall's real, that it's strong enough, that it'll hold.

"Bad karma," Shirley says. "I knew it. The one day you catch me looking at the wall, the next I'm sick as a dog. It makes sense."

"Come on, Shirley. Nathan's sick too. I never showed him the wall. He'd have felt the same way about it as you."

"I still say it's karma. Reap what you sow."

"What'd you do with all the pictures?"

"Gone, poof, sacrificed them to fire. Right there in the sink."

"There could've been fumes," John says. "You might've gone up with them."

"Didn't think about that." Shirley's looking around inside her handbag for snacks. "My boys were so sick. I was cursing your name all night. I was going to phone you and have you clean up the mess."

"Just be careful next time."

"You're right," she says. "I get so set on purpose, I forget to think."

"Me, too," John says. "It happens to the best."

Nathan calls off work the whole week. The doctor says Nathan's just suffering from a flu, gives him tablets to settle his stomach. Still Nathan's listless, doesn't speak. Dishes collect in the sink. John's half afraid to leave Nathan alone during the day, but Nathan, in what words he does give, says all he does is sleep. Nothing else. "I sleep all day long. I'm saving my energy, be back on my feet in no time."

The little energy Nathan does possess seems to be spent in the morning lovemaking, more passion than John has ever felt from him. Nathan cries out, pained, and kisses hard. At times, Nathan's love, his ravenous appetite is too much. John closes his eyes to avoid Nathan's face, his look that means "it's time." On top of it, John feels flabby, heavy, he hasn't been running, spends his spare time napping, restoring order. Nathan's loving hands seem to seek out the parts of John's physique that've softened, as if gauging the slackened upkeep.

What the hell. With Nathan sick, John needs no excuses, no lies. Nathan sleeps—maybe not comfortably and peacefully but still lost in the world of the safe unknowing—so John drives to the nearby exit of the turnpike, close to the river—a rest stop without adequate light that keeps the deservedly hidden, hidden. Nathan's driven him to this anyway, hasn't he?

John keeps the car unlocked, a fast get-away possible should the police show up—though they never do, never here; quite possibly the law can't even guess what goes on at this off-ramp.

A clustering of trees begins just beyond four locked bathrooms encased in brick. John follows a slight, trodden path down into these woods. The earth is soft and compliant beneath his feet. Sticks snap; he's not alone walking here.

In the dark, they are all faceless, unimportant, the first will do. John nods. The man nods. John motions him to follow and he does and soon they are in John's car, John's fly is open and he is pushing the man down. Does it matter if he has a face at all? Isn't it enough to become familiar with the back of this man's head, his wispy dark hair, how he is large and smells of mayonnaise and knows exactly what to do. When it is over, John says, "Thanks." The man slides from the front seat of the car. John won't look at his face, only the back of him, his camouflaged hunting vest as he walks up the path and becomes part of the vegetation, blends into the woods.

John's not sure how he feels after what's done is done: satisfied, invigorated, content, appalled, disgusted, relieved. Why does he care? Yet, driving home, he narrows his choices to glad *he did* and wishing *he hadn't.*

This is John's first run in days. Nathan sprawls at the center of the bed, a sheet twisted between his legs. John covers him with the comforter, tosses an extra blanket across for warmth.

Outside, the morning rain is slight, though the weatherman's predicted a warm and sunny day. The drizzle grays everything, blurs it shape. The houses along the road are no longer so clearly defined. Leaves whipping around on trees seem to congeal, mix, it's difficult to tell where anything begins and ends.

His legs are stiff, stiffer than ever, and he blames the lack of exercise, the rocky nights. He pushes himself harder, the macadam slaps under his feet—and where the road is less sure, in need of repair—gravel shifts, scratches.

This morning, he knows what it means to be back at the house. When he thinks of Nathan home sick and in bed, John does feel something of guilt, a heat pushing through pores in his skin that makes him want to stop, need to stop once he reaches the house, its orange roof, the cats staring at him from the open mouth of the refrigerator. He slows. There. Someone is home.

A man comes forward, takes one step and then another from the porch, the cats swirling about his feet, their tails flick-flicking the air. John hears the mewing. Halfway through the yard, at the place of the gardens, the man stops. He is short, short for a man, and grossly overweight. His yellow T-shirt and worn trousers can barely contain him, his large speckled arms, his flat and fat bald head and brightest blue eyes and the spurts of dark hair spiked up behind his very small ears. He looks like a father, someone in the position to judge. "Good morning," he says. Or he doesn't. John stares at the man's lips. They could be saying anything.

"Good morning," John says. He feels suddenly ashamed, giving those words so easily. The man smiles. The garden about his feet looks unforgivingly ripe, beyond sweet-tasting, trampled down, the colors of the vines' fruits too bright. John watches the man take his hand and reach slowly inside his own pants. His hand catches on his stomach as he reaches down between his legs. One of the cats is trying to crawl up the man's pant-leg, shoving its orange head under the cuff. The man scratches himself and retracts his hand. John pretends he's wiping his brow, catching his breath, and he runs, not slowing down even once the house is lost behind him.

Nathan's just awake when John reaches home. The room is hot, still smells of vomit not properly cleaned. "You don't have to do anything," John says and rolls Nathan onto his back, slides a pillow under his head. Nathan begins murmuring, nothing whole comes out, just gibberish, and John places his mouth over Nathan's, pushing with his tongue, just to get Nathan to shut up for a while.

Now guilt has a face. The plague he's avoided: someone must know. Throughout the day John keeps thinking of that old man, expecting that horrible visage to appear in one of the photos he develops. Every time the blown-out whiteness of film paper acquires eyes, mouths, noses, John sucks his breath.

"You're acting weird," Shirley says. He shrugs her off, pretends she's not even there. He's made a ghost of her, sees right through her until he sees nothing at all. He'll do this to all the customers, every empty-faced one that appears before him. He no longer lives in their world.

A headache stretches like a cap over the round of his skull. As the day wears on, he grows sluggish. He's started feeling sick himself.

"Let me drive you home," Shirley says after work. "I can pick you up tomorrow morning. Your car will be safe in the lot for one night."

"No, no, no, it's not necessary," he says.

"I know it's not necessary."

Shirley's pushiness, it's too much, but he can't fight her. In fact, on the way home, he's glad she's there, with him, his paling and failing strength. He tells her how sick Nathan's been. She gives John a look like she already knows. Neither judgmental nor approving, her eyes linger over him. He can almost see sympathy pooling there in her eyes, in the moment of twinkling that comes before tears. She's always been overly touched by pain, why it has to exist at all.

"So everything's under control?" Shirley asks. Bangles on her arm clatter. How unnerving the sound. "You're A-okay?"

"What?"

"What."

The foolishness she's alluding to, whatever she's balancing on the tip of each word, he can't handle it now. He closes his eyes, helping the ride home to go faster.

Walking up the lawn, to the house, despite John's pleas of non-necessity, Shirley says, "I get bad feelings already." Before going inside, she stands in the doorway, sniffing.

Nathan's nowhere to be found, not in any room, not hiding anywhere. John and Shirley go into the backyard, calling his name. They spy him, dressed only in boxer shorts, sitting alone at the picnic table under the draping tendrils of wild-cherry tree. "Yes, it is a beautiful day," Nathan says. "It looks like rain again."

How embarrassing Nathan's near nakedness, Nathan's now thinner body sitting so poised and postured at the picnic table. John and Shirley step closer. Nathan turns. "Join me," he says. His hair is slick, pasted against his forehead. Patches of his skin look chapped. He places photographs in front of him from an open travel pamphlet, dealing them as if he were Judgment and they a fortune deck. He places each snapshot with such emphasis, as if to say *this one, now this one, now this one.*

Before anyone can understand what John's done, the lawn-chair flips, Nathan lies sprawled in the grass, blood seeps from his mouth. John's staring at his own fist, clenching his forearm with his free hand, studying it as if his own body were some invention he'd only stumbled upon and, by accident, made work.

Shirley runs for the house, almost as if she knows the threat, now done, has passed. Nathan feels for the ground beneath him, pushing himself up, wobbly, to his feet. When Shirley returns, with a wet cloth and ice, she packs them to the side of Nathan's mouth. She upturns the plastic chair, steadying Nathan into it once more. John wishes someone would say something, offer some explanation or condolence if only to break the tension that has hoisted itself over and above the yard like a red tarpaulin. But no one speaks.

Staring at his feet, the earth, clay, grass, pebbles, tiny twinges of motion from a grasshopper leaping into a safer unknown on its spindly legs, John paces the perimeter of his property. Minutes pass. Shirley crosses the yard to where he stands. She puts her arms around him, a hug, yet not, rather a pulling together, as if all of him would dissociate and disperse had it not been for her force.

"Take him for a drive, for fresh air," Shirley says. "Keep him warm." John knows what it means for Shirley to say this to him now, to let him in the care of Nathan after what he's done. For the first time he realizes that Shirley understands better than he does what exists between him and Nathan, what has existed for some time.

John wraps Nathan in a comforter, doesn't bother to dress him, puts him in the front seat of Shirley's car and locks the door. He drives to Tysonville and back, almost to Gettysburg and back. The night trickles in. Fewer and fewer cars populate the road. Nathan sleeps the whole time. His breathing changes from rapid to slower patterns, more comfortable and pleasing ones. On the way home, John pulls the car over to the side of the road, stares out into a cornfield, and without waking Nathan, holds him. He touches the reddening and swollen side of Nathan's mouth. Able to appreciate the harm he's caused, John kisses it, then restarts the car.

When he and Nathan return home, two hours later, the house is spotless, the dishes returned to their proper shelves, the smell of sickness gone. "Why didn't you tell me? That it was this bad?" Shirley asks. The air conditioner's on, cooling not chilling the place. Both Shirley and John tuck Nathan into bed. Color returns to Nathan's cheeks. His toes curl and uncurl. His condition will improve, slowly, little by little, then in leaps.

"She'll take care of you both," Shirley says. John isn't sure if she's speaking of herself in the third person, or if she's referring to some higher, even sweeter power.

A little before midnight, Shirley leaves. "I'll pick you up in the morning," she says. "Expect things to change."

Left then with the quiet of his and Nathan's house, the plaintive company of the refrigerator's hum and the air conditioner's reply, John goes into the backyard. The photographs have blown, the naked images that occupied his thoughts and assisted lusts and escapes have blown. Some have stuck themselves to the chain-link fence.

Away from the house, from the dangling branches of the wild-cherry trees, he sets fire to each of the photographs; one by one, before flames meets his fingertips, he tosses the burning pictures to the air. Such a simple gesture really. They fall so heavily, burn quickly, like small but dazzling comets to earth, releasing smoke that seems blacker than the night sky.

Already John knows that Nathan will leave in the morning, that Nathan will avoid him, not take his calls, will make him suffer and pay for days, for weeks maybe, until finally Nathan—faulted by his own ability to forgive—will bend, cry into the phone, "I miss you." "I miss you, too," John will cry back, because there is nothing else he can say, because he knows no other words, and for Nathan, these words will mean more than one thousand apologies. For weeks, months, John will try, honestly, to keep things as he knows they should be. He will wear guilt and humility as if they were his proper attire. His body will give way. Within a year, he will suddenly feel old. He will allow himself finally to love Nathan as Nathan loves him: shamefully, honestly, desperately.

John slows passing the house. It feels good to be running, though he still feels out of form, like his body is someone else's he's just trying on. But he realizes the energy's still there, that the muscles have not atrophied. It's all in his mind.

John leaps up the front walk, not slowing, even for the cats that tumble wide-eyed at his feet, trying to trip him up, divert his attention. He runs to the front door, notices letters, past-due notes that have overstuffed the mailbox. The ink addresses have smeared. Old Coupon Clippers are forced under the doormat that's missing letters, presumably ripped off and played away by the cats. *WE OME* the mat reads.

John knocks. There's no sound, only the passing sound of the old house. He pushes the door open, expecting a family to be sitting in the living room, mother and father and sister and brother accusing him for entering their old house, for casting it into the state of abandonment which it now suffers. He can half see them, for just a second sitting in the regalia of their day, their time in the sun, but they vanish, are only figments of what he assumed would be waiting. In fact, there is nothing, not even a sofa to sit on, nothing to prove that the house was ever lived in or loved by anyone.

what is now proved was once only imagined

The backyard was lit with mist and moon and the puckering glow from faraway porch-lamps brought Miriam's anger further forward as she recalled the glare of the Bingo Bazaar and losing to Ed when she was just one number away: G54. He hadn't understood why she'd been so mad. She hadn't either but there was no denying the spark that shot straight up from her gut and out toward her teeth and toes and finger bones. "A windfall's a windfall," Ed had been dumb enough to say. Even after the drinks he'd bought her for forgiveness, she'd told him to go. No part of her wanted to risk sneaking him into her bed tonight; no part at all. And now, to make matters worse, the yard was drenched, almost a swamp the way it squished beneath her.

Lost in a tide of whiskey sours and feeling all of her forty-four years, she remembered: she'd left the water on.

A dog barked nearby, so many of them around, sometimes breaking their chains and quietly terrorizing the neighborhood, ripping open trash set out for morning pick-up, spilling garbage. Nobody needed to see what she was throwing away. It was like being touched when you didn't want to be touched. But what was worse? The dogs chained and barking all night long so she couldn't sleep or the dogs running free and silent and ripping open Hefty bags?

Along the length of hose, the holes she'd punched with the iccpick spit out small fountains. The petunias and scarlet sage— that normally looked up at her open-mouthed and expectant like the children she tended weekdays—were heavy-headed, bowing down. From the wisteria, burdened white blossoms had fallen and lay in an incomplete circle around its twisted trunk. With all the water in the air, this dew and the humidity, the scents of so many flowers were caught and held captive, mixing one on the other, putrid and nauseating, so she couldn't be sure which it was—the smell or the burning in her stomach—that made her whip quickly at her waist and vomit, just missing the marigolds.

Night seeped in. She swung open the door of the garden shed, trailing the hose that snaked up a sink to where it screwed into a rusted nozzle. She cranked the faucet. The water stopped.

From above the sink, moonlight blazed through a spidery-cracked window. Everything cast in this framed diamond of window light looked drained, bloodless: blanched flowerpots and unused tulip bulbs lined up along shelves, a trowel staked into a mound of potting soil, the crumbly dirt floor. She held her head; something harsh and triangular felt as if it'd lodged behind her eye. She blinked, once, twice, again, again. Her eye beginning to tear, she looked up and squinted, startled by the man in the open doorway of the garden shed.

The dull blue of the neighborhood behind him, he hovered effortlessly, at comfort, above ground. Air somehow supported him. He was neither young nor old. His hair spiked outward like a crown and was short and maybe a little blonde but she couldn't tell, couldn't begin to tell because of the light. A deep robe, not a bathrobe, a choir robe with its loopy sleeves, was draped over his body which she knew was gaunt and drawn thin with pallid skin and boils and pussing sores. Scars stretched across his forehead; they were trenched deep in his brow and in the shapes of things one might see carved into trees: tic-tac-toe games, *CR + ML FOREVER* trapped inside a jagged heart. Nothing made sense. His eyes looked gouged out and burned. His mouth was a mistake. He didn't look like anyone at all.

The man undulated in striations of vertical light, slow patterned beats, a heavy flash and then one less so, main impulses and afterthoughts. She tried for words. None came, or if they did, she had moved beyond them, for the heaviness of her mind now stretched thick and tarlike into her stomach.

The man rose along the door, holding his arms in a loop above his head. The sleeves of his robe slipped down over his wrists and lower, revealing those loose elbows. He joined hands, fingers gnarled into fingers as if they couldn't do it quick enough, as if they'd been trained and waiting, stretching and twisting, pulling like roots. Miriam reached for a hoe, broom, something, but when she did, the man before her frowned. His lips turned suddenly bumpy and segmented as earthworms, and then he was no longer there.

She might've blinked, for now she stared out into the blue of the neighborhood. A dog still barked. She couldn't move from her spot for some moments, wondering if somehow she'd gotten trapped in one of her own dreams—those that came when she did sleep—heavy and blanket-like, tucking her in too tightly. She pinched herself to realize this was happening after all and pushed open the window above the sink, hoisting herself up and out and snapping branches from a rhododendron when she fell to the ground on the other side.

Somewhere the wind blew. She heard the tin chimes. The moon had come fully from behind a cloud, and she could see where large puddles of water had collected in the lawn. Her mother would complain tomorrow when the already hot June sun would burn the grass dead.

Miriam climbed the back porch, saw the muddy tracks her socks were leaving. There'd be no hiding it. She'd have to set her alarm and wake early, before work, before her mother, and scrub the porch down. She looked back to the garden shed; the door hung open: a gaping empty mouth.

She left her clothes in a pile and stood naked and cold at the center of the kitchen. Chrome appliances gleamed from their dark corners. She ran her fingers across the blender; it seemed so strange a thing.

Taking the stairs to her room, turning, she looked about when the smallest creak or crack would pull at her fear; the slightest shift of a shadow became an event. Under her feet, the fluff of the carpet was comforting. That, at least, she knew was that.

When she encountered her mother at the top of the stairs— her mother's face laden and blued by shadows and the pale light coming through so many windows—Miriam felt herself falling backwards, saw actually in her mind her own crumpled form lying at the bottom of a staircase. Miriam's hand forcefully clutched the banister.

She couldn't tell if her mother was awake or asleep. The old woman's eyes were barely open, if it all. "I know what you're up to," her mother said.

Miriam looked down at herself, at the parts of herself she could see in the darkness—her naked sagging breasts, the stomach that normally rode over the stretch-waist of her pants. "I don't know what you're talking about," she said.

"You're a drunk."

Miriam went into her room, climbed under the pilled summer quilt draped across her bed. Her mother had moved to the doorway, standing now hands on hips. "She's shrinking," Miriam thought, remembering photographs of her mother, how each photo, moment to moment, year to year, showed her mother getting smaller, shoulders inching toward one another, pulling together, collapsing as with a drawstring on a laundry sack.

"I saw something in the garden shed," Miriam said.

"It's hard to believe you take care of children—"

"I know what I saw."

"The way you go about—"

"Mother—"

"What kind of standard is that?"

Miriam let that boil inside her. She wouldn't look in her mother's direction. She focused instead on the child's mobile dangling from the ceiling of her room—ceramic seagulls flew at each other and then away. She rolled toward the window, looked up at the sky. The window needed cleaning, but Miriam turned the streaks and smudges into clouds, stationary clouds that floated in vast flatness. There was nothing else she could do tonight, nothing at all. Things out of place would stay out of place, no moving back the stone to cover the hole now.

Her mother remained. She stood in the doorway for several long seconds, neither of them speaking. Miriam didn't face her, not even when her mother retreated, creaking across strained floorboards to her own room. Soon the old woman's snores fluttered through the house. They were nothing really, only snores, but as Miriam listened, these snores became everything. Just like that, they were everything in and outside the house, the barking dogs, the trash bags, the horrible thing that appeared to her in the garden shed, and she was thinking, as she fell to sleep, that these snores would be there once she'd given way to dreams. The snores would be there, whether she could tell they were there or not, and she was frightened by the idea of time continuing, of lives existing without her, more than she'd ever been, ever on any other night.

The raspberry preserves turned liquid. She couldn't steady them on the knife, they dripped across the tabletop, sometimes onto her toast. She'd been thinking too much, realizing then, in the morning, that he, it, whatever it was, had come for her.

She watched her mother go about the backyard, examining the flowers, lifting blossoms. Their colors looked too bright now, unexpected in the sunlight. Her mother wore a hospital gown—a small ribbon tied the back—and her straw gardening hat with green beaded doodads dangling from the brim. "You really did some damage last night," her mother said. In her hand, as if an offering and evidence, she held three tiger lilies. Sap puffed from the stems.

"I'm late," Miriam said. "I know what I saw."

Miriam didn't expect her mother to believe her. What her mother thought didn't matter at all, shouldn't. Anyway, what was important was whether or not the vision would come again. She wouldn't allow herself to call the thing "a ghost." That seemed not quite right, for it had been some sort of vision; it had chosen her for a reason.

While the other day-care girls were at morning coffee break, Miriam took her turn watching the children at outside recess. They played such queer games: Murder Ball, Deer and Hunter, anything to do with death.

Now she watched the children aged five and six, twenty of them. They looked alike, limp-haired, wild, thin more or less, except for Ellie Windsor who Miriam let sneak cookies from the snack table. Thinking about these children, Miriam imagined what each would look like in upcoming years, how their bodies would change and their spirits would change—for the good or bad—shaped and shaped and reshaped. She'd not seen her own son in ten years; he'd turn twenty-seven this fall. He'd been such a good boy, and then, suddenly, was not, wanting nothing to do with her. Like most people in her life—Charlie, the boy's father included—he'd slipped away, orbiting Miriam and her life at some unseen distance. She hated her son: for who he was, for his anger and stubbornness, for the snapshots he would send at Christmas and a hurried note whose information seemed scatter-shot and incomprehensible, she could barely make sense of his life. At meal times, each evening during her bath, she would think of him in Georgia, Florida, wherever he happened to be that year, and awfulness would envelop her in this net: that he would not be thinking of her as much as she did of him.

She was careful the day-care kids didn't climb the fence. They were always trying, digging little sneakers into the perfect fit of the chain links and hoisting themselves toward the top. A main road was nearby. She'd envisioned car crashes many times. The child lay in an oval of his or her blood, head cracked open, the wound in the shape of a jagged frown. There'd be blood on the car, splashes across the grill, maybe even the windshield dabbed with what looked like finger-paint. Things like that could so easily happen. One night, after work, after drinks after work, she'd been driving home—it wasn't too late yet—and that boy had come out between cars parked along the road. He'd been chasing something, a ball, a cat, something. Before Miriam could stop, she remembered thinking—practicing was it?—*Yes, it's my fault, it's my fault, yes, yes, it's my fault.* The boy's face hadn't shown fear.

He was smiling as the car neared him, caught in the middle of a joke or funny thought as Miriam slammed the breaks, jolted herself, the boy, the world to a halt. The boy waved, ran into the road after whatever it was he was after, not once forgetting to smile, never stopping to think that anything outside his life would want to take it away.

Miriam tugged a chocolate lozenge from her pocket, watching five girls play London Bridge—a ninny game—in the corner of the day-care yard. "Take the key and lock her up, lock her up."

Sunlight fluttered the top of Miriam's eyelids, dazzling, turning. In the center of this light, she could imagine what she'd seen last evening, the vision. Now it was only a replica, some small thought caught in her eye and her brain, but she could again see the same drawn out face, the head shaped almost like a bucket, wide at the top and narrowing to chin. She could see the thick hair, darting out, chaotic and threatening, from the man's head.

A buzzer sounded, her recollection dispelled.

"Okay, time's up," she shouted. The children chased each other around the yard. "Okay, time's up," she said again. None seemed to be listening, so she let them have five more minutes at play.

It was no surprise: Ed standing in the lobby of the day-care, holding flowers. He was in uniform, white shirt, blue pants with industrial keychain, on break from reading electric meters for the local utility company. Under the fluorescent lighting of the lobby, his bald head glistened harsh and pink. His unshaven face, his blue eyes that floated too low in their sockets made Miriam remember, despite her current hatred of him, that he was someone she cared for.

"I'm at work," she said.

"These are for you."

Miriam took the flowers, irises. She didn't smell them or smile at them or even say, "Thank you" and wouldn't want to say too much due to the nosy receptionist listening, and once she got hold of anything, any story, she'd change it somehow, say people did things they hadn't done at all. "I was hoping we could get together tonight," Ed said. Miriam knew what that meant.

"I have a special project to do this evening."

"Maybe you could come over later?"

"What would I tell my mother?"

"You're a grown woman for Christ's sake."

"It's not that easy. She needs me."

"No she doesn't."

"I don't want to talk about it here." She handed him the flowers and walked back toward the lunchroom. The receptionist, a two-time divorcee who smoked vanilla-scented cigarettes, was leaning against the windowglass of her cubicle. When she saw Miriam, she pretended to be studying a sheet of paper. Miriam knocked on the glass. "I sleep with him," Miriam said.

"That's nice," the receptionist said. "Everybody needs somebody."

"How would you know?" Miriam said. "Are you everybody?"

The receptionist blushed, knocked over her can of pencils and purple pens.

Back in the lunchroom, among the lights and the complaints of silverware and the caterwauls of her co-workers and the shining white-board across which someone had markered HEY DUDE, WHAT'S UP?, Miriam thought about what she'd said to that woman she barely knew. She wondered where the strength to say something that up front—to anyone—had come from.

If she could recreate the scene, the vision would find its way back, she thought. After dinner of corned beef hash and shoofly pie, she just needed to get out of the house. She said she was going for a walk, to the corner store. Her mother looked at her suspiciously. "What's at the store?"

"What's not here," Miriam answered.

It took her five minutes to get to the bar on the corner. She stopped only once to read a poster proclaiming a young girl lost, a $5,000 reward pending information regarding her whereabouts. The poster was stapled to a telephone pole with thick industrial staples. The top staple went through the girl's head.

Miriam didn't go often to the corner bar. Normally she hated drinking in public places, alone. The bar was small with a jukebox and video poker-machine that was OUT OF ORDER. Whatever else was there, Miriam didn't want to know about. She sat down at the bar, bought a shot of whiskey, and then another. If her mother wanted a daughter that was an alcoholic, Miriam was convinced she could be one. She downed the drinks as fast as she could order them, six shots in thirty minutes.

"Rough day?" the bartender asked. She didn't look up, didn't even want to know what he looked like.

"I'm getting my vision back."

"You don't look blind to me."

"How would I look if I were?"

The bartender walked to the other end of the bar. "Cuckoo broad."

It was getting dark when Miriam found herself stumbling along the edge of the main road, back toward her house. When she passed the telephone pole, she stopped again to read the flier about the lost girl. This time she laughed and grabbed the flier from the pole, shredding it, letting the pieces flutter to the ground. She kicked some of the scraps into the street, tripping over her own shoes, almost falling into an oncoming car that looked like nothing more than its headlights.

What little was left of the sunlight stretched out pink just above the stark outline of trees beyond the few houses. She watched the night slowly covering the light, attacking it like a wave on a shore, only the night didn't recede and rush again at the light; it kept coming.

From the road, Miriam could see the flicker of the TV through the front window of her mother's house. She could see the back of her mother's head, bobbing forward and back in the rocking chair. Miriam went to the window, knocked, then ducked behind a bush.

When her mother looked out, Miriam jumped from behind the bush and waved. Her mother clutched her heart. "You're going to make me have an attack," her mother said.

"I'm sorry," said Miriam, pressing her lips to the windowscreen.

"Ed called while you were at *the store*. I told him you were out. Get in here before somebody thinks you're loony."

Miriam felt her mother's looking and dissecting. "There's something I don't like about him," her mother said.

"Ed has a job. He's steady."

"Steady with the electric company? That's new. Since TMI, the company's going nowhere but underground."

Miriam went to the kitchen to peel an orange. Her mother kept talking, so Miriam went even farther away, out the back door, and sat on the screen porch, listening as crickets poured from crevices with their screeching. A dog barked. Things were settling or unsettling. Water sprayed from the garden hose, drenching the backyard and the flowers. Her mother had decided to water. The sun hadn't scorched the lawn after all.

"I'm going to sleep," her mother said at nine o'clock. She paraded out to the garden shed, in flip-flops, and as Miriam watched the old woman disappear into the shed, her heart kicked. She wasn't sure what she was expecting. "Mother," she called. The water flowing from the hose trickled, trickled and stopped.

"What is it?" her mother said, coming from the garden shed, with the same admonishing look she'd always shot off when Miriam was a child, like when Miriam went too far from the shore or talked to just any stranger on the street. Her mother's look of irritation and judgment: its power to melt away, diminish and dissolve any conviction Miriam had worked for.

"Never mind," Miriam said.

"I wouldn't want to be you now. You're going to have a headache—"

"Do you love me?" Miriam asked.

"What a silly question."

"This is important."

"Miriam, if you want me to say you've had a hard life, I will. Things have not always been easy for you, and if you've been waiting for someone to say that to you, I'll be the one. There it is. Now I'm going to bed."

Miriam heard the window fan upstairs. It whirred and whirred above her, and the way she felt, she thought it might fall off its ledge and onto her head or possibly send the house into flight, it was so loud. She liked that: a little flying house just looking for a place to land. She tried remembering her mother's words exactly—they'd sounded so pretty and right coming from the old woman at that moment—yet already they were lost, mixed up.

Miriam stared at the garden shed. She hadn't gone near it, chancing it in daylight would have degraded the night before. Now, the darker the night became, the more the shed seemed not itself. The walls looked as if something inside were pressing against them, threatening their seams. She watched this for an hour. Then she stood, walking across the yard. Mud squished between her toes.

Inside, the garden shed smelled of the waiting it acquired every summer, how moisture would get trapped under the roof and mix with wood and rot. Miriam walked toward the sink, cranked the faucet, even though the water was not on. She turned, only to see the open door, the garden path made of seashells and white stones weaving in and out of flowerbeds.

Miriam looked at her watch. It hadn't been that much later the night before. She waited, she waited. A car stopped in front of the house.

She peered through a crack in the shed's wood wall and recognized Ed's car, a four-door, blue and gray Pontiac Sunbird. Ed came around the side of the house, large and rocking in his T-shirt and cut-offs, and stopped at the edge of the back porch, examining the trellis of morning glories that crept to the second story. He tested the trellis with his hand, started climbing.

"What are you doing?" Miriam said.

Ed turned, his grip loosened, and he fell the three or four feet to the ground, stumbling backward.

"I was coming to see you," he said.

"You were going to climb to my window?"

"I was going to try."

"You'd have broken your neck. What a sight that would've been."

Though she wanted still to be angry at him, she kissed him. He kissed her back with something that was not the intensity she had hoped for. Instead, his lips touched hers with tenderness, embracing hers, not forcing them apart. She stepped back to look at him.

"I saw something in the garden shed last night."

"What?"

She thought of explaining it to him. Though she didn't know what she was explaining exactly, she felt an authority, as if she professed to knowing this one thing, those who did not know would have to believe her. She took his hand and led him up the steps to the back porch.

"Your mother's home," he said.

She shook her head. "She's sleeping. Just be quiet."

They climbed softly up the hall stairs to her room. The netted curtains flowed out like sails, drifting across her bed and creating sheer, crisscrossed shadows, small grids of motion. There was barely time for them to undress. She held her hand over his mouth as his body moved. She thought about the vision, how it'd appeared and easily disappeared, was there and then not. How different Ed was from the man who'd appeared, the man with scars and his thin pallor, his deathly or dead appearance. Ed filled her arms with all of his body, but for a moment, just a flash, she imagined making love to the man from the garden shed, that saint or spirit. She placed a hand at the top of Ed's head, touching along his neck, to a solid place where the shoulder bones met.

Afterwards Ed closed his eyes to sleep—and though she knew he could never spend the night here—she let him sleep and pushed her head into the warm pocket at the center of his chest. She felt her dreams coming, leadened and heavy, things were unfolding, long dark garden plots filled with flowers and roots that ran from their soil and obscured the garden path. She was settling into something, the alcohol, the sleep, somewhere between, when the light of her bedroom went on.

The old woman stood in the doorway, crazed, her hair ratted, her one cheek red and patterned from where it pressed into the zipper of her pillow.

Miriam sat up. Ed sat up beside her. "What is it?"

Her mother turned. The bathroom door slammed. Miriam heard sobbing. "God, I'm sorry," said Ed. "We shouldn't have done this."

"Let her go," Miriam said.

"You should've just come to my place."

"She had to know."

"I'd better go."

"Go if you want then," Miriam said. "You would have eventually." She looked at the small freckles dotted across the upper slope of one of her breasts.

"I came here for you," Ed said.

"I know."

"Isn't that enough?"

"Maybe not."

He dressed quickly. Her mother still cried behind the bathroom door. After Ed left, Miriam felt, for once, as if she'd done everything right. For once she was happy, a moment, and then, as she came back to herself, immediately sad. She stood and looked from the window at the garden shed. It was silent and glowing under the moonlight. She lifted the windowscreen, picking one of the dormant morning glories from the trellis beside her window. She found the place where petals overlapped and forced her finger under, pushing open the blossom with the point of her thumbnail. "Mother," she said. "Mother, come out of the bathroom. If you slip and fall in there, how'll I get in to help you."

Maybe it inhabited some place. Like a genie, she thought.

Under the guise of cleaning the garden shed, she collected things from the soft interior of the wood shed and dragged them out into the garden. She found things she'd not imagined to be hidden away: a red tricycle missing the front wheel, a broken gramophone. Mice had burrowed through headlines of old papers—NO END NEAR FOR WAR, JFK SHOT—and squeaked at her as she lifted the reams of newsprint. She'd always liked mice and felt bad destroying their home.

She carried the forgotten objects into the garden, rubbing each thing in hopes of releasing the vision, the spirit. It was silly, but it seemed somehow necessary. Like losing twenty dollars at the mall. There'd be no hope of finding it, yet you were always compelled to revisit all the stores you'd been in, hoping always for a miracle, a good Samaritan.

"Are we having a yard sale?" her mother asked. She came into the shed when Miriam was bent over three cans of beets she'd found in a corner under the sink.

"Spring cleaning."

"It's June," her mother said. Miriam tossed the cans of beets into a large, red bucket. "Make sure you don't trample flowers."

"I'm not going to trample any of your flowers."

"You say that now . . ."

Miriam pried things from the soil, pieces of broken glass that had been pressed down under feet or wheelbarrow, small bottle-caps, things she let fall casually into the trash bin. There were brass buttons, a buffalo nickel, several plastic barrettes. Once everything had been cleared from the shed and sat looking back at her from the garden—as if she'd created her own dump in the backyard—she asked herself what she'd been looking for. What it really a magic lamp? Was that what she expected to find?

"Have yourself some lemonade," her mother said. "I never realized we had all of this stuff packed into that tiny shed." Miriam's mother seemed worried, her bottom lip was rolled up into her mouth. "This was your father's." The old woman held a small magnifying glass that centered a dot of sunlight on the grass. "He'd always use this to read."

"I remember," Miriam said. "Of course, I remember."

"I guess you didn't find then that thing you were looking for. A boogey-man, was it?"

"No, I didn't find that thing. But it was there," Miriam said. "It was there. It came for me."

"You've always been one to imagine disaster. If things happened the way you pictured they would, we'd all see and believe things that weren't true. We live in a true world, Miriam. You should know that by now."

"Maybe I'm not a true type."

"I hope you aren't planning on throwing this stuff away. It's too painful to have everything moved. I want it all back in the shed where it belongs. Some day I'll want to look it all over. But not now."

At the Bingo Bazaar on Friday night, Miriam sat on the opposite side of the room from where she usually sat, even though a woman wearing a daisy in her black hair gave Miriam the evil look. Miriam knew about bad luck. A move in the Bingo Bazaar was cause for alarm. The slightest shift from routine channeled all vibes, good and bad. Everyone knew that. It came with the territory.

Ed sat where he usually sat, two beers placed in front of him. He hadn't noticed her. Miriam set her vinyl blotter bag down on the corner of her seat and pulled out the green and pink and blue blotters—Kermit, L'il Sue, and Jasper. The orange, purple, and yellow ones (Tabor, Ruthie Jean, and Romeo) she left stuffed in the pouches of the blotter bag. She took L'il Sue and marked the free spaces across her ten bingo cards. Before the game started, Miriam bought herself a Bud Lite and a Miller Lite from Ms. Vincent, the vendor. She liked drinking one half of one and one half of the other and then pouring the halves together.

Smoke clouded the air—cigarette, pipe, cigar, even incense from the tie-dye hippie who always brought her two screaming kids. The numbers flashed onto a TV screen as the caller announced them. A man with a transistor radio held to his ear was listening to a horse race. "And they're off." Miriam looked over at Ed. Between every number, he'd scratch his head as if puzzling a mystery.

The man wearing a sombrero won the first game. "BINGO!" he shouted, his voice cracking on the O, but everybody was too busy complaining about how close they'd come to winning to hear him. Miriam watched Ed hard at work, stamping his blotter against his cards, marking them like if he didn't have the blotter he'd be slamming his fist against the table.

The second game went to the one black woman who came Fridays for bingo. She sat where there was never enough space. People'd look at her like she was crazy. She wore jangly bracelets. Miriam sometimes wished this woman would sit next to her, but she never did.

The third game, four corners, was won by Old Bill. Everyone called him that, "Old Bill won again!" and somebody'd slap the table.

The caller started the fourth game—postage stamp, four in the upper right corner—and Miriam found herself stamping spots, watching the clock more than anything and as much as she liked the bingo, she didn't want to be here tonight. She finished the beers, savored the mixer of one and one, and numbers came, random, everything so random. She looked down at her cards. She saw the four squares, marked pink by L'il Sue, clumped together in the upper corner of one card. Just like a postage stamp. On a letter ready to be sent. It wasn't something she could believe: her winning now. She checked her numbers with those already called. She didn't want to be wrong about her winning and upset everybody. No, she wouldn't want to upset anyone, but she checked and double-checked and was right. The card was right. She felt hot and nervous, and for a second, considered not calling, maybe somebody else should win, maybe somebody else needed it more, and she looked at the ceiling, at the yellow ceiling and the visible rafters and slow turning ceiling fan as heat washed down and out through her. "Bingo!" she yelled, the word sounding so strange in her mouth that she doubted it was she who'd said it. But it was because everyone was staring. She kissed L'il Sue, jumped up and down—Ed turned to look—and she went to the caller table to claim her prize: $500.

"Thank you, thank you very much," she said. She held the money in her hand, out so everyone could see, she knew they were jealous she was there holding the prize and they'd got nothing.

The woman with the daisy in her hair stuck out her tongue.

"Maybe I'll win a second time tonight," Miriam said.

She walked one mile from town, saw the houses she knew so well and the bar and now trees, marked with white paint, waiting to be chopped down. The highway was expanding soon. There were trees, all alongside the road, stiff slopes of trees and green that rose slowly along hillsides turning to gray, then grayer to black to blue to deepest blue. The lights of a Mobil station advertised FOOD and FUEL. Miriam entered the small convenience shop and handed the slow-faced boy behind the counter a twenty-dollar bill. She held out the whole wad of her money, so he, specifically, could see it.

"I wish I had some of what you got," the boy said.

"You do? Give me quarters, all quarters."

"I don't have that many."

"Then give me whatever you have."

The phone booth was outside the station. Miriam wedged herself between the uprights, heard the quarter slide and land inside the phone. She dialed Ed's number.

"Let's go," she said, when he picked up.

"What?"

She pressed down on the receiver, called him again.

"Let's go," she said.

"Where are you?"

She hung up, dialed him once more.

"Let's go." She was about to hang up again.

"Yes," Ed replied. "Let's go."

"This is where you'll find me," said Miriam, and when she'd told him, she opened her hand, spinning the three remaining quarters the slow-faced boy had given onto the macadam.

She stumbled over a guardrail, hugging a thick maple for support and kneeling beneath a tree marked with a white X, right where an axe was meant to clear it for the expanding road. A jagged heart had been carved into the bark, two sets of initials, forgotten.

From where she sat she could see down the road into the town of Sinking Springs. Her mother would be winding the clock. Dogs barked. Soon Ed would be along to find her. She thought of Ed, her lover, driving, imagined the lights playing across the road, fanning the gas station parking lot, to suddenly find her, squatting again beneath this old tree. Imagine the sick glare of those headlights: how they'd seize her.

The five hundred dollars was a warm lump in her pocket. She looked down at Kermit, yellow Romeo, Jasper, L'il Sue, Tabor, Ruthie Jean. A passion washed over her like death. Clutching the bingo-bag tightly, Miriam started to run. She'd guide them through the night. She wasn't fast, but she kept it up, knew she had to, because if someone did show up this time, she shouldn't be waiting.

miracle-gro

Peet Hillegass had been thinking all morning about too much of a good thing being poison, so he decided to try it. In the supply shed behind the church, he took one white industrial-sized bucket, filled it from the tap, and emptied an entire box of Miracle-Gro. The water turned a shocking shade of blue. He heaved the bucket out into the sun and toward the cemetery. By now, he knew exactly where all five hundred forty-seven were buried and how long they'd been there. "Head Maintenance," Peet called himself. The janitor/groundskeeper who'd held the position before had suffered a massive heart attack, an unfortunate result of strenuous labor, and left the spot open. Peet had jumped at the opportunity, spending the weekdays of the past seven years wandering the empty church, straightening hymnals, playing at the piano when no one else was around. He worked the cemetery as if it were his own, something he could memorize and that made complete sense.

With the concoction of Miracle-Gro, Peet walked among the headstones, the row closest to the highway, and stopped when he came to a rose-marble marker. BERTRAM CHASE, it read. A picture of a deer's head was etched beside the name. Peet put down the bucket and imagined his former dentist there, lying beneath him. The afternoon Peet remembered most was when he and his father had gone into Bertram's office—Peet recalled being about ten—and Bertram's breath had smelled like medicine or a whiskey. "You're going to be a mush mouth for sure," Bertram had said. "I can read it in your teeth." The words had been a curse. Every time Peet went to the dentist now—the new one, Dr. Milkin—he would lie back in the dentist chair that felt more like a medieval torture trap than anything, and he'd have to endure that horrible drill as it rammed and rammed and rammed into teeth and gums, leaving him a mouth full of blood. No matter what he did—he brushed twice each morning, twice each night— his mouth was filled with rot. Had Bertram kept quiet, Peet might've been looking in the mirror every morning at a set of perfect ivories, not a mouth filled with snaggled teeth and stains and a decay he could not exactly see but knew was there. Peet tipped the bucket so a portion of the Miracle-Gro splashed across the grass of Bertram's grave and waited while the water seeped into the ground. Then Peet smiled and spit and hurried back four rows, over seven plots to ELAINE MENSCH.

She lay under a white-marble-cross model that made it seem she was a saint. He pictured her: hands clasped on her chest and decked out in a lavender knit. She was one of those who always wore some purple. Normally, Peet would've just pissed on his old teacher's grave, doing figure eights with his urine stream, imagining her shriveling up her nose up at the smell, but today he had the Miracle-Gro and dumped some of it over her plot. She'd made his fourth grade year a living hell, telling him once—after sticking his face in the corner of the classroom—that he wasn't going much further in the world. Now look at me, Peet thought. Now who's calling the shots?

With the last of the Miracle-Gro he doused out BARB WORTH. She'd been good cause to break that love thy neighbor clause, tattling to Peet's parents and anyone who'd listen all through his high school years about what Peet was doing and with whom. She'd turned on her porch light and caught Peet and that girl screwing in the middle of her yard—that was the worst of it. Peet splashed the Miracle-Gro over Barb's grave and imagined the hissing of acid as the fertilizer bled into the ground. He could barely wait to start seeing results.

Following the barbed-wire fence that framed the cemetery off from a pasture, Peet made his way back to the church. A cow forced her heavy head through the fence to chew at the greener cemetery grass, and when Peet came close she didn't move, but looked up at him, her visible eye upturned and revealing the soft cusp of pink muscle along its edge. "Get," Peet said. The cow didn't move until he was very close, and even then she rolled her thick tongue out to grab at more grass before retreating. She'd have taken the fence with her if the barbed wire hadn't let go of behind her head where it'd dug in. The fence posts shook and the barbed wire snapped and rang like the whole thing might come undone.

He took the bucket back to the shed and was locking up when he heard voices coming around the side of the church. It was Monday after all, which meant nobody was supposed to be around. During the week he looked at the church like some vacation house a rich person might own: opened up every so often to let out the foul smell and cared for by invisible servants the rest of the year. But now, the voice of Reverend Willow Peet recognized right away; it was too much like the burble of a quail.

"There you are, Peet," Reverend Willow said. He was pear-shaped and had a sprig of hair sticking up like a pull-tab at the back of his head. Beside him was a woman at least the reverend's size, except her shoulders were broader; she was wearing bib overalls. "Peet, I want you to meet . . ." The Reverend paused and looked at the large woman beside him. "Claris? Is that it?"

"Claris," the woman said. She downstroked her finger on the first syllable. "Like in 'Claris a bell,' my mother said."

"Yes, that's right. Peet, Claris Holler. She's a young lady from the program I told you about."

Claris had her hair pulled up in a bun that sat too far forward on her head. She looked thirty-five and her ears stuck out and she had the biggest grin Peet had ever hoped to see. Really she didn't look so different from the yellow smiley-face earrings she had dangling from her ears. And Peet remembered her. She was in fact a small celebrity in the Sinking Springs area. She'd robbed houses and stolen cars before finally being arrested.

"This was my first choice, I want you to know," Claris said. She was holding her hand out. Peet just stared at it. She smiled even more and let her hand fall to her side. "I'm ready and eager to work."

"I think you two will get along," Reverend Willow said. "Peet has always done such a good job himself, but with building on to the church in a few months, a second body's going to be welcomed."

"I'm real easy to get along with," Claris said. "Just mold me. You show me the ropes and I'll be an excellent worker."

"I'll show you the ropes," Peet said, then he looked to Reverend Willow. "But we were expecting a man."

"Women need acclimating into society, too," Claris said. "I was only away for five years and already I feel like I'm living in another time. You know, it's like I'm Cinderella except I get plopped down in the middle of the Civil War? Or like I went to sleep one night, and the next morning I wake up and the whole world's changed, people have flying cars. Something like that."

"I haven't seen any flying cars," said Peet. "Not much changes around here if you don't let it."

"I don't mean real flying cars."

"Well the other day, I thought I saw one fly right over the church."

"Oh, I get it," Claris laughed and turned to Reverend Willow, slapping her hands together. "The joke's on me. Anyway though, I'm not from here originally. I was born over in Lemoyne, but now some friends of mine have me set up in a little co-op kind of arrangement right over a shoe hospital. My little saying is that if I ever need a heel healed, I don't have far to walk."

"I'll let you two get to work," Pastor Willow said. "Peet will take good care of you." He nodded and shuffled quickly around the side of the church. What kind of business could be so pressing with God on a Monday?, Peet thought.

"So where do we start?" Claris asked. She'd reached into her pocket, pulling out a handful of hard candies. "Want some?"

"First, we start with rule number one."

"These are a little sour, but I like them that way."

"Rule number one: I work best by myself, so I can't deal with talking all the time."

"Oh, mark my word, Peter Hillegass, I'm gonna fit into your world. We'll be working and talking, talking and working. I'll just get in with you like we're a well-oiled machine. You just watch me."

"Peet Hillegass."

"What?"

"Peet. My name's Peet."

That afternoon they cleaned the sanctuary. Peet would've sent Claris off by herself right away, but Reverend Willow told him to stay with her for at least the first few days. She'd been in prison, after all. Peet didn't know what Claris would want to steal around the church—maybe the offertory plate or a hymnal so she could start her own religion. Pastor Willow had said, "Doing time doesn't erase the act. It only clouds it with a begging for forgiveness."

Claris took her finger around the ledges at the front of the church. "Look at all this dust," she said. "You'll be glad I'm here."

Peet turned on the vacuum cleaner and ran it down the red carpeted aisles. She kept talking—he could tell from her moving mouth—but he didn't hear a word.

Claris picked up the golden rod the altar boys used to light the Sunday candles. She held it in front of her, looking at it as if it were magic, and then she started marching back and forth across the front of the church. Peet stopped the vacuum cleaner.

"I always wanted to be an altar boy," Claris said. She'd extended the wick from the one end and walked from candle to candle, pretending. The way she wielded the thing, though, made it look as if she were preparing for a fight. Her motions were so hard and fast she reminded Peet of a Kung Fu fighter.

Claris put the candle rod down and approached the pulpit. "Welcome, everyone. Welcome to God's door. I am the way and the light." Then she burst into laughter. She looked up at the ceiling, then at the large portrait of Jesus hung over the altar. "Sorry, God. I was just joking. You know me, Claris."

For a moment, Peet thought, "Is this happening?" He started wrapping up the cord to the vacuum cleaner.

Claris eyed the piano. "I don't see how you ever get anything done," she said. "Working here's going to be so much fun." She ran her fingers up and down the keyboard. Then, beginning with the highest, she played each key individually, all eighty-eight, until she had gone from high to low. She changed directions next, beginning low and singing along this time. Peet couldn't remember a more horrible sound filling the inside of a church.

When he got home, there was a letter from his mother and father. They took turns writing to him; one week his mother wrote the letter, the next was his father's chance. They only lived twenty minutes away, but they thought it brought them somehow closer. When Peet was going through his "angry years"—as his mother called them—his parents had left notes and letters all over the house, each one of them filled with words like *loving* and *dedicated* and *proud*. In the letter that just arrived, however, his mother was asking him to come for dinner on Sunday. His sister Dorris was going to be visiting from Pittsburgh. Peet crumbled up the letter and stuck it in his pocket. He'd considered the scope of his world to be very small, which never troubled him really, except when his parents or visiting Dorris and her popgun-shooting bastard child Charlie threatened to make it even smaller.

On Peet's doorstep, someone had left a Dixie cup filled with walnut meat. He knew it had to be Mrs. Aver because when he looked up, one of the yellow curtains in the middle of her trailer fell back into place. The old women of Peet's trailer park, Scratch Acres, were always doing things like this, leaving anything from sandtarts to casseroles to knitted gloves on his stoop. Sometimes they'd deliver the goodies themselves, but Peet would keep the old women on the other side of the screendoor. Peet ate one of the walnuts. It was bitter, almost tasteless; he remembered why he didn't like nuts and dumped them into the aluminum garbage can.

Inside his trailer, Peet looked around at empty Jiffy-Pop bags, the videotapes and magazines he'd left scattered across the floor. Things never seemed to find their proper places.

Something smelled. Fetch-It, Peet's beagle, had done it again.

Peet saw the stinking mess in the middle of the kitchen. "Occasionally the muscle—the sphincter—tires out and can't hold back anymore," the veterinarian had said. "Everything comes out. The dog doesn't have a choice." Peet remembered Fetch-It looking up at him from the long metal table in the vet's office, the dog's eyes saying she was already defeated. Peet tried not to be angry, but he couldn't imagine not having any control over something like shit.

Fetch-It was under the bed, where she usually lay shamed after she'd done the inevitable. Peet threw dirty socks at her, and then cleaned up the mess—the whole trailer reeked of it—so he cranked open the windows, even the little one over the toilet that was crusted shut with mildew.

He started to sweat and took a beer from the refrigerator, popping in one of the videotapes, a porno remake of *King Arthur*. He sat down on the sofa, propped himself up as usual between pillows. Two slow sips of beer and the video began. Even though the acting was bad, the voices excited him. He could pause them in a middle of a word, fast forward and rewind, all by pressing a small button.

"I hope you can save our kingdom," Guinevere, dressed in a leather bustier, said.

"I think there's something else that needs saving." Sir Lancelot kneeled before her, his eyes the level of a huge padlock hanging between her legs.

"What could that be?" Guinevere shook her hips. The padlock bounced, two times.

"If thou highness wouldst permit me to showest?"

Fetch-It wandered into the living room, wagging her tail. She stopped in front of Peet and farted. "Get," he said, but Fetch-It didn't. She lay down at Peet's feet.

Guinevere was naked now, stretched out across the Round Table. Sir Lancelot stood behind her. The movie set had been made to look like the inside of a castle: block walls, stained glass windows, wrought-iron chandelier. Peet noticed a light switch. "Look at that," he said.

Outside the trailer came the irksome sound of a car idling, loud, like the muffler was about to let go. Then he heard steps coming down the walk. He zipped himself up and lowered the volume on the TV.

Bing-bong, bing-bong, bing-bong the doorbell sounded. He inched back a curtain. Standing on the cinderblock porch was Claris. She was holding an Easter basket.

"Peter Hillegass? Are you home?" She'd raised her hands like a bullhorn to her mouth. He let the curtain fall and slid down against the wall, pulling in close like she might look in a window and see him.

Fetch-It started to bark. She didn't get up, just sat where she'd been sitting, and barked.

Peet could hear Claris reasoning out the situation. "His truck's here." Then she walked away for a bit, then came back to the door. "Maybe he's asleep or something." She rang the doorbell again. She moved around the porch, looking at things, opening the hood of the gas-grill and closing it with a clunk; he heard her sliding the welcome mat. "I guess I'll just leave it."

Something was going on. It was quiet and he was afraid to look, but when her car engine started, kicking several times before it finally caught, he stood up and watched Claris go. "Woman Driver," a yellow placard said, hanging in her car's rear window.

Inside the Easter basket was a leather wallet that looked used, a baseball signed by the Baltimore Orioles, sugar cookies in a green Christmas tin, five red apples, and a small scribbled note on the back of a bank receipt that said: *from Claris.* He sat on the sofa, turning over the contents as if they were shells, checking to see what might be hiding underneath each one. Fetch-It nosed around the basket, sniffing and huffing.

On the TV screen, Sir Lancelot was parleying with the Lady of the Lake. He might've been asking about the Holy Grail. Or, just as easily, he could've been asking for something else. Peet put the basket to the side of the sofa and turned the volume up.

He got to the church early the next few days to water the graves with Miracle-Gro. By Thursday, the grass over BERTRAM, ELAINE, and BARB had started to brown at the tips and was working its death slowly toward the roots. Anyone viewing the three plots, charred and brown while the rest of the cemetery flourished in green, would've taken the marked plots as a sign from some higher power.

Claris never said anything about the basket. And he didn't bring it up. He tried to keep her working alone, sending her into the bell tower if he were in the basement of the church. He ate his lunch on the run, wolfing down whatever sandwich he'd made and the Hostess cherry pie with a can of Mountain Dew. "I don't eat lunch, usually," Peet told Claris when she asked, so after that, if he wanted her, he could usually find her sitting in her car, staring at her sandwich as if she were waiting for it to speak.

When Peet happened to walk past Reverend Willow's office one day, Claris was in there, eating. Reverend Willow probably wanted her to join the congregation. Peet stopped by the door and listened.

"Before, I never understood how a person could give as much, like preachers and such, always giving and smiling—"

"—well, we all have our moments of selfishness—"

"—but I have this feeling and I'm wearing it like clothes, but on the inside."

"I know what you mean."

Claris talked with her mouth full. Peet could imagine her shooting out food at the reverend. She liked egg salad, lots of yellow egg salad that somehow got smeared over her lips and cheeks while she ate. "There are a lot of bad ones out there," Claris continued, "preachers included, but I think we all need to just come up against evil."

"Evil?"

"Yep, the big E-V-I-L evil. I used to be bad, and now I'm making myself good. Hey, where's your wife do her grocery shopping?"

"At the SuperFresh."

"See, maybe there's something to that?"

"I'm not sure I know where you're going, Claris."

"Well, you see, your wife shops at the SuperFresh. I shop at the Giant. Now what does that say about us?"

"I couldn't guess."

"Neither could I, but I'm sure it says something. Everything says something."

"I guess so."

"Yes, everything sure does."

Peet covered his ears and walked away shaking his head. He walked into the broom closet and, with the light off, stayed there until his lunch hour was over.

Later that same day he saw the hose snaking its way into the cemetery. "Stop," he yelled, threading through the headstones, following the path of the hose. Claris was standing over ELAINE, pressing her thumb against the lip of the hose so the water splayed out like petals from the center of a flower. Peet looked at the ground, the dry grass glistening with water. He imagined ELAINE beginning to stir, nourished and rejuvenated, her dead hands regaining life and struggling against the red clay and black earth that buried her. She wanted back into the world, would be stronger than before despite Peet's effort to keep her memory down, dismissed and tucked away.

"What the hell are you doing?" He grabbed the hose from Claris.

"Some plots out here are dead, Peter. I just thought I'd go ahead and water them."

"Did you ask me?"

"Three plots were dead. Some animal maybe did its business on them or something."

"I said, 'Did you ask me?'"

Claris looked down at her feet, around at the surrounding plots as if the answer were to be found there. "Well, no, I didn't, Peter—"

"Did I tell you to water these plots?"

"No, but—"

"I'm in charge here, right?"

"Right."

"Then you don't do anything without asking—"

"Ah, come on, Peter. I was just helping."

"You help too much."

Peet could almost feel the dead grass turning under his feet, Claris's water weakening the slow poison of his Miracle-Gro. He dragged the hose back toward the church. Part of it had looped around Claris's foot, tripped Peet up, and when he turned, Claris looked caught in the middle of some emotion, her mouth gaped, open and ready, like she'd been knifed suddenly and gutted. Small licks of hair strayed from the bun on top of her head, and at that moment, Peet thought he'd never hated anyone more in the world. The intensity was hot in his chest, like a lump of coal burning inside to out, releasing fire and red energy and light. Claris stood in the middle of the cemetery, the hood of her bright pink windbreaker flimsy and flapping at the breeze. If she was expecting an apology, she wasn't going to get it.

Normally he would've just gone through the drive-thru, but for some reason the Hardees workers seemed to handle you faster if you went inside. "How can I help you?" the girl with the crooked name-tag asked. She had a small birthmark, a burn or scar maybe, on her neck. Peet pictured her standing over the deep frier, the grease popping and fussing and burning her skin.

He told her what he wanted—it took her a while to locate the buttons on the register—and then, when the total came up to be $32.85, she said she must've done something wrong. "This is my first day," she said.

"I bet it is."

Peet gathered ketchup packets and mustard, some sugar, too, he knew he was out of sugar. The whole restaurant was a mess, used straws and napkins all over the floor. He budged his head around the corner into the dining area. It was mostly geriatrics like the ones who lived in Scratch. They lifted hamburgers and french fries slowly to their mouths, as if they had all the time in the world. So much for *fast* food.

He was turning, didn't think anything really of the pink vinyl mass sitting in the corner by herself until she looked up and started waving. He would've run if he hadn't been so shocked.

"Hey, Peter," Claris shouted. "Sit here." He hadn't talked to her since earlier that day in the cemetery, thoughts of BARB, BERTRAM, and ELAINE conquering the prospects of thinking anything else. Clearly Claris was an extension of their will, but in the living world. In the corner booth, waving arms, flapping like a big pink bird, Claris shouted again. Obviously any hurt she might've felt had worn off.

"I'm taking mine home," he said. "See ya."

He went back to the register and finally the girl had figured out something. She handed over a bag of food.

"Yeah, this place isn't good for atmosphere." Peet turned to see that Claris had picked up her tray and was standing behind him. "I'll just come along with you." She rewrapped the food on her tray and lifted a stray onion ringlet, slurping it between her lips. "I knew you had to eat sometime, Peter. No way you could stay so strong and not eating anything."

"I gotta go."

"I'll follow you back to your place."

"I'm going to have company."

"Oh."

He pushed his way out the glass door, skipped almost across the parking lot to his truck. Claris was still inside the Hardees. She glanced down at her watch, then at the floor as if she'd dropped something.

Peet let the truck roll. The tires turned underneath him, out of the parking lot, past the church and miles of barbed-wire fences. Three boys were hanging in the sagging wild-cherry trees by the trailer park entrance. The kids pelted the truck with the small, ripe fruit when he passed under them.

Mrs. Aver waved from her porch. It looked like she'd wrapped a twig through her short ratted hair, but when Peet got out of the truck, he could see it was some brown ribbon.

"Have you been visited by any good spirits lately?" she asked.

He just wanted to get inside. "Good spirits?"

"Fairies. You know, good souls leaving things for you to find?"

"No," he said. "I think you've been skipping pills again."

Fetch-It didn't greet him at the door. Peet expected a mess to be someplace if the beagle was hiding, but he looked and looked and couldn't find the dog or anything she might've left behind.

He spread his food out in the middle of the floor: two cheese-burgers, fries, Dr. Pepper. He'd just turned on the TV when there was a short buzz of a motor outside, then the recently too familiar sound of shoes stomping down the walk. Claris's face appeared in the window of the screendoor. His first reaction was to play dead, maybe she didn't see him, but she didn't stop at the door. She pulled the door open. She came inside, carrying her fast food held firmly in her hand, as if the bag were a briefcase and she the double agent delivering top secret information.

"You made me feel bad today, Peter Hillegass. I think we should both apologize to one another."

Peet looked at all the video tapes lying across the floor. Claris picked one up. It was as if she'd touched his most personal, private thing. He wanted to grab it out of her hand and conceal it with a pillow.

"You must like videos," she said. She sat down on the sofa, springs loosened inside, and there was a low yelp as Fetch-It came crawling from under the sofa skirt. She looked hurt, the way her back leg dragged, but when she stopped and saw Claris, Fetch-It turned the other direction.

"Oh, you've got a pet," Claris said. She grabbed Fetch-It by the collar and pulled the dog back into her thick arms. "Nice puppy."

Peet looked at Claris sitting so easily on his sofa, as if she'd made the place hers by just being in it. He went to the kitchen to get a six pack. If he was going to get through this, he was going to get through it drunk. He started moving some of the video cassettes into a pile, pushed others under the sofa when he thought she wasn't looking.

"You're not orderly are you?" Claris said. "That's usually how it is though with people like us."

"People like us?"

"Yeah. We take care of other people's stuff and treat our own like shit." Claris loosened her grip on Fetch-It's collar and the beagle bolted back down the hallway. "Fast dog."

She bit into her burger and chewed. He couldn't help thinking she looked like the cow that was always eating at the cemetery grass from the other side of the barbed wire fence.

"You should've seen me back before I decided to be nice," Claris said. She stood up, put her hands on her hips and then pantomimed drawing two six-shooters. "Pow, pow." Then she put her hand to her mouth and looked at the ceiling. "There's a spider over there in the corner." She grabbed a napkin and hopped onto a chair on the other side of the living room. "I'll get the little sucker."

"So you were a real bad girl?"

"The baddest. Sometimes I took people's cars. Just for drives. I never did any damage to the cars I'll let you know, though I admit I did take some hi-fi equipment once or twice. That stuff I never could give back, even if I wanted to, because it was out of my hands about as soon as it was in them. You might've liked me better then." She smashed the spider and the napkin into a tight ball.

"So now you're reformed?"

"Things don't ever go completely away. How about one of those videos?"

"I don't think you'd like them. Sort of boring."

"I've seen all sorts of films and liked them all. Sometimes I think the idiot-box and the movie theater were invented with me in mind."

"No, let's not—"

"No problem. I got it." She grabbed a cassette from the floor and slid it into the VCR. She flounced onto the sofa. The cushions sagged beneath her. Across the TV screen, a man and a woman— their legs and arms pretzeled around each other's bodies—rocked across the floor of a yellow room. "Holy Jesus," Claris said, taking a bite of her hamburger. "I've never seen it done that way." She kicked off her shoes and settled back into the sofa.

It was getting dark outside. Already crickets were starting to whir, the fat inch-long crickets that pulled themselves from the damp earth beneath the trailer. Claris kept staring at the TV, taking small bites at her sandwich. "Don't tell anybody," she said, "but I even killed a man once. I'm not proud for doing it. I never told another soul, but I thought you should know." Peet listened to the words come simply and effortlessly from her lips, as if she were telling him she liked chocolate or preferred red to green. *I killed a man once.* "I buried him by a railroad bridge, chopped him all to pieces. It was self-defense, of course. He's better off anyway."

Claris slid off her socks and started inspecting the space between two of her toes. Peet looked at her, her pale eyes in what light still came through the window. Her eyelids quivered as she talked. Her nose wrinkled suddenly. "What's that smell?"

He was thinking of finding that railroad bridge. He could see it so clearly: her in the cast of the moon, her flesh the color of dead flesh. Would she be crying as she pushed the shovel into the soil? No. She would be so incensed, focused, her bun undone, possibly the smiley-face earrings dangling from her ears. She would be surrounded by the low humming that belonged to nothing but the night. And then: a distinct sound, something separate, a crack. She would turn to look at the line of trees on each side of her. She would look down through the bridge, at the black water, and then up, at the sterling sky where there would be the moon but no stars. What was that sound? Something fast approaching? He saw her rolling the body into that vast ditch. It would be wrapped in a shower curtain or stuffed into potato sacks tied with curlicues of binder-twine. And she'd fill the hole, shovelful by shovelful. She'd be talking to herself, thinking of the flowers and grasses that would grow from this one bad thing. Yes, that was it. Too much of a bad thing. If too much of a good thing were poison, could too much of a bad thing be anything else than undeniably good? Peet pictured himself there at the railroad bridge—present time—taking the shovel, digging and digging through the wild peonies and blue chicory that had flourished, concealing the crime. He'd dig until the shovel faltered and struck bone and then he'd wipe away the dirt and the worms and the roots that'd claimed the flesh and the blood. He'd balance the dead man's skull in one hand, looking into hollowed sockets. In that black emptiness, he'd find himself. BERTRAM, BARB, ELAINE, too. And he wouldn't have to think of them ever again.

"What *is* that smell?" Claris said. Peet knew what it was—the smell of something letting go, putrid and disgusting, invading the trailer. But he couldn't figure out how to tell her, because looking at Claris and how she filled his couch with all of her body, he knew he'd never be strong enough not to love her. She was his for life.

hydra

He remembered seeing it first a few days before, a vague gray mass moving across the sky with the bloom and pulse of a jellyfish until it paused and fell gently into place over the house, as if it meant to stay, for a while. When he'd looked more closely, he could make out individual fibers, rising and falling in the thin breezes that drew music from the tin windchimes on the porch. No one else seemed to notice. That first night, the rest of the house asleep, Henry stationed himself by the bedroom window, thinking about the strange swarming fibers until his head began to hurt. He hadn't ventured to touch them, but something drew him there, some hidden presence coursing through them. And for a reason that he couldn't explain, Henry was sure that in a day or two, the small weblike fibers would somehow loosen themselves from the house and everything would be revealed.

He detected a whisper—faint, rushing at him and confused. The sound seemed to correspond to a pattern the individual fibers were playing against the window glass, a systematic tangling and unraveling, and he was certain he was on the verge of figuring that out.

"We're busy," said Henry. "Can't you see that?" He turned to his mother, then to his younger brother who sat rigid-still in front of the television, tapping the control pad of his Sega Genesis.

"Your aunt and uncle are here," his mother said. "Help them unload. They drove all the way from Erie."

"There's not enough room for them in this house."

"We only need a few adjustments," his mother answered. "Please help them."

Outside, Uncle Dale and Aunt Shirley stood to the side of their Pontiac, figuring the best way to lower their possessions from the car roof without everything falling on top of them. Uncle Dale circled the car a few times, spit once at the tires, and rubbed his forehead; Aunt Shirley held the Twins like plump flour sacks in her arms; and Little Alexander, the three-year-old, was clamped at Aunt Shirley's pantleg, staring as if there were nothing behind his eyes to process what he was seeing. Henry couldn't resist making a horrible face that sent Little Alexander burying his head into his mother's rear.

"The whole family's come to greet us!" cheered Uncle Dale. He turned, stuck his thumbs into his pants-pockets, smiled.

"I had to wrestle them out of bed. You remember Henry, and this is Jess. Twelve and nine," the mother said. "Henry's the smart one, Jess is full of energy."

"Aren't they big boys," Aunt Shirley said. "They are big."

"This one looks like a beer drinker." Uncle Dale poked Henry in the lump of stomach that pushed over the top of his shorts. "Are you a beer drinker just like your daddy?"

"I'm not old enough to drink beer."

"I remember that night your dad and I got a case of Rolling Rock and we sat there in that Amishman's field and drank it all, one two three. When we staggered in, your mother and your aunt were at the kitchen table on fire."

"That was also the night we locked you both out of the house and the two of you froze to death," Henry's mother said. "Anyway, I don't have time for stories. You're two hours later than I expected, and I'm already late for work. Move your stuff into the empty room at the top of the stairs. You might find some of Russ's things left behind, but that you can box up or shove out of the way. We'll figure out where the kids will sleep when I get home."

"Okefenokee," said Uncle Dale. "What've you boys been up to all summer?" Uncle Dale took a container of chew from his back pocket and rubbed a pinch between his lip and gum.

"Ick. Not in front of the children," Shirley said.

"They're boys."

"Well if not for them, then think of your own children." Shirley walked to the other side of the car. Little Alexander followed, dragged.

"Want some?" On his stained index finger, Dale held out a small mound of chew.

"No thank you," Henry said. Jess pinched his nose and shook his head.

"I'll make men of these boys. Let's see how we're going to get this stuff down off the car."

Henry looked at the lawnchairs and a laundry basket and the old red bicycle that Uncle Dale had tied to the roof of their Sunbird. He wondered how they'd made it all the way from Erie.

"I have to admit this is some rigging on my part. I didn't have much to work with—some binder-twine and a little nylon rope. How about I cut and you two stand on the sides to steady anything that falls."

"It's all going to fall. I can see that already," said Henry.

"Let's just try it like Uncle Dale says and see what happens, okay? It'll work."

Henry stood on one side of the car with Jess opposing him, hands out, ready to catch anything that might tumble from above. Henry held firm to the bicycle that seemed most likely to fall fastest and hardest.

"Okay. One two three." Uncle Dale cut through the first cord with his pocket-knife. Everything held place. Then Uncle Dale cut cord number two, number three, and then before Henry or anyone else knew it, the small mountain on top of the car shifted in Jess's direction. Henry could see his younger brother gripping at the lawnchairs with all the strength in his thin arms to keep them from sliding. But the chairs were already on the move, down and over the windshield. Aunt Shirley was screaming from the safety of a tree.

"Hold it," said Uncle Dale. "Hold it." And Jess didn't let go. He looked up, red-faced and relieved he'd prevented any of Aunt Shirley and Uncle Dale's belongings from hitting the ground.

Uncle Dale sprang to the front of the car. "What's that? What's that there?" Uncle Dale pointed to a slight metallic scrape that ran halfway across the hood of the car. "You made a scratch."

Jess stretched to see, then nodded.

"Is it such a big deal, Dale? Really," said Shirley.

"He stopped it from falling," Henry said. "No one will notice the scratch anyway. There's lots over here."

"What's done is done." Uncle Dale spit on his fingers and rubbed them back and forth across the scratch, expecting it to go away. When it didn't, he shook his head. "You two are going to pay me back for this somehow," he laughed. "Ha-ha, I'll have you work it off."

"Pay for what?" Henry let his side of the pile go. "It's just a scratch."

"Pay for a new paint job that's for what."

"You'll be paying us for letting you live here."

"So, it comes down to that, does it? You won't talk to your father's brother like that. I don't care whether your pop's run off with some whore or he's lying in a rat-hole pissed out of his head, you don't talk to family like that."

"He hasn't run off. He just hasn't come back," Henry said.

"Dale!" said Shirley.

Not far beyond Uncle Dale, the fine silvery threads trespassing the house shivered with each word. Not yet so far beyond.

Uncle Dale hoisted the bike and lawnchairs from the roof and leaned them against the side of the car. He told Jess to put these in the shed. Henry wanted to help—knowing he and Jess could curse their uncle once clearly away—but Dale stopped him with a large pink suitcase lifted from the trunk. "If you please, sir . . ."

Once all of Dale and Shirley's things had been lugged to the waiting empty room, Henry returned to the front porch, looking for Jess. Upstairs, Aunt Shirley sang to the Twins in a brassy operatic voice. Uncle Dale was bent over at the door to the backseat of the car, gathering up dark brown bottles from the floor. He clutched them to his chest—some of them upside down, some right side up—as if they were his own desperate children who'd been gone so long he could no longer tell which end was meant to be kissed and which was meant to be spanked.

Henry grabbed the bag of Oreos from the cupboard, and he and Jess stole away to the cornfield so near their house. Aunt Shirley had already commented on how her and Uncle Dale's room was much too small for their needs; new arrangements would have to be made. One of the Twins succeeded in vomiting on the other, while Little Alexander watched everything with the same empty look.

"I bet that one's retarded," Henry said, biting into the first Oreo. "He doesn't look right to me." Henry took another bite.

"Give me one." Jess reached his hand into the bag and pulled out four, stuck three in his pocket and put the remaining one in his mouth.

"Uncle Dale isn't very much like Daddy. I don't see how they could ever be brothers. Look at you and me—we're pretty much the same. Except for some things I'm better at than you, but that's just because I'm older. In three years, you'll be as good as I am now."

Jess had set up two rows of stones in a shallow furrow and raked a clear path between the lines with his fingers. "I'm building a city," he said.

Henry stretched out his foot, kicking over the first stones in one line. "Are you listening to me?" Jess pushed Henry's foot out of the way and started over.

Henry took another bite from another cookie, and was chewing, thinking of the dark wafer and the white cream separating. As he reached for another, he heard the sound of hooves against asphalt.

Jess looked up from the city he was building. "Horses," he said. Then he was off running through the rows of corn, his head bent low. Henry grabbed the bag of cookies, stopping to pick one up when it fell to the ground, and followed after Jess. Henry couldn't keep up. The crescent-shaped leaves of the cornstalks licked at his bare arms and seemed to cut more severely the faster he went. Eventually, he reached Jess, squatting like a frog among the high grass at the edge of the highway.

A black horse and buggy were coming on slowly in their direction. Henry could make out the driver with his black hat and black trousers, his white shirt tucked in tight around the waist, and the grim riding crop in hand that the driver sometimes used. The horse was the shiniest black and, depending on the way the sun caught it, the horse's coat would glimmer in traces of red and brown and deep purple along its mane and back.

"Steady," the driver said when the horse became edgy from a passing car. Blinders kept the horse on course.

"He's alone again today," Henry said, eating the cookie he'd rescued from the field. "I wonder why he's always alone." When Jess didn't answer, Henry looked to see the egg-sized rock his little brother was juggling back and forth in his hands. "Are you going to hit the horse? You should hit the horse. When it jumps, that Amishman will be scared more than the horse."

"I don't want to hit the horse."

"Well, if you can't do it—"

"I can, but I don't want to."

Jess stood up and let the stone fly. It hit the horse low in the stomach, causing the horse to rear up against its tether with a high-pitched whinny. The muscles in the horse's neck and legs bulged. The Amishman tried to guide the horse to keep it from charging across the road.

"I told you I could do it," Jess said.

When the horse calmed, the Amishman leaned to the side to see what had startled the horse so. Jess shoved his thumbs into his ears, making faces at the man all in black. "Get a car!" Jess shouted. The man's face shriveled. Without a word, the driver turned and continued to usher the horse at its slow pace along the highway.

"I told you I could hit it."

"You're a pretty good shot," Henry said. "Dad said you'd be a good pitcher for the Little League. Maybe I'll practice with you someday if I have time. There's a lot of stuff I have to do before then."

Henry watched the black spot of the horse and buggy until it became part of the blue horizon at the end of the road. When the bag of cookies was gone and the sun was a heavy orange ball,

Henry said they should go home. Their mother had definitely returned and maybe order had been restored.

"I'm going to stay here until that Amishman comes back this way," Jess said.

"I said we should go."

"I don't know why I have to listen to you," Jess said.

In their absence, the weblike strands that'd overrun the house had multiplied and become more distinct, swollen almost like overboiled spaghetti noodles and seeming so easily volatile as if at any moment they would merge with one another or burst or else detach themselves from earth and take heavily to flight.

"You see those threads, don't you Jess?" Henry asked.

Jess shook his head. "You're seeing things again."

The closer Henry came to the house, the more he realized that what he'd originally thought were small threads were really living things. They were thicker now and wormlike and warm, stretching their many-headed bodies all over the house. He could hear them breathing, each inhale and exhale causing what anyone else would call a breeze. When he came nearer, they raised their gray heads and seemed to look at him with their sweetly translucent blue eyes, which made him think of trying to touch them. He could feel the inviting warmth these living things gave off, but drew back when they tried to meet him halfway.

"The Twins have to sleep in me and Dale's room," Aunt Shirley was saying. "And Little Alexander I don't want too far away in case he gets lost. One night he wandered into our apple cellar and we found him balled up in the corner the next morning, cold as ice."

"Well," Henry's mother said, "we could put the boys in the room I'd planned for you and Dale. But that means moving everything around. It'd take a while."

"But, really, wouldn't that work out better? Dale doesn't have a job yet, so this'll give us all something to do tomorrow and Sunday. The boys will help I'm sure."

"I don't see why Jess and I have to give up our room," Henry said. "We live here. This is our house."

"It's for the Twins," Aunt Shirley said. "You can't have me and Dale and the Twins all in that room. On the other hand, it's just big enough for you and Jess to be comfortable."

"All I know is that I live here, and I don't have a say."

Aunt Shirley spoke through her smile: "Henry, it's the least you could do after scratching up Uncle Dale's car."

Henry climbed the back stairs to the second floor. He could hear Aunt Shirley commenting on what a self-possessed young man he'd turned out to be. Henry would've gone into his room, slammed the door so the whole house would know he was alive and angry, but there Uncle Dale had passed out face-down in the lower bunkbed. He snored from deep within his chest, and it seemed to Henry that he was not about to awaken for a very long time.

After dinner, Henry changed the bedsheets and put a new pillowcase in place of the one Uncle Dale's face had touched. "I like my things clean and tidy," Henry said, to no one in particular, though he thought Jess was listening. "Uncle Dale smells like beer. He reeks of it. I don't know how anybody could sleep smelling like that."

Jess was on the top bunk, mouthing words at the pages of a Superman comic: the one where Superman gets married.

"You've read that thing about a thousand times," Henry said. He fluffed his pillow and stopped for a moment to admire his work. "Let's do something else that the both of us can enjoy. If you want we could pretend you're Superman."

Jess turned the page.

"Or better yet we can think of things we could do to Uncle Dale and that family to show them. I would think of the plans, and you can help out. Do you want to do that?"

Jess closed the comic book and reached between his bed and the wall where he'd hidden a small bag of cornchips.

"Where'd you get them?" Henry said.

"They're mine."

"No they're not. They're mine that I hid in the drawer. I was looking for them today."

"You eat enough," replied Jess.

"Back to Uncle Dale and his family." Henry sat down at the small writing desk and took out a pencil. "Let's see. What should we do?"

In each room of the house, there'd been at least one of them: the Twins screaming from their bassinet, Little Alexander shoving anything that wasn't tied down into his mouth, Uncle Dale drooling, Aunt Shirley noticing the things she'd like to help change around her new house. *Henry could see the silvery wormlike creatures stretched over the windows of each room, seething. He could see them now, just barely beyond the bedroom window as he sat down to write.*

"If we could think of something."

Little Alexander came into the room. He took a few steps, catching his foot on the rug, and fell forward.

"What are you doing?" Henry said. "This isn't your room." Jess looked up from the comic book he'd reopened and was interested enough to slide from the bed.

"Hey Little Alex," Jess said, picking the boy up and shaking his arms. "I think he wants to be like us."

"He doesn't want to be like us," Henry said, but when he looked this time and saw the solid emptiness behind the boy's eyes, he changed his mind.

Little Alexander crawled across the floor, picking up the pillowcase his father had slept on. He lowered it over his head, then lifted it off again.

"He wants to play peek-a-boo," Jess said. "Peek . . . a . . . boo."

Little Alexander pulled the pillowcase over his head and laughed.

"What we should do, for his sake, is tie him up in that and throw him in the river," Henry said. He went over and tugged the pillowcase as far down on Little Alexander as it would go. Then he held it tight around Little Alexander's legs. "All we need is some rope. We'd be saving his life."

Little Alexander moved his arms inside, trying to get out.

"Let him out," Jess said.

"He looks like a little ghost," said Henry. "If we keep him in this a little longer, he'll be one for sure."

"Stop it!" Aunt Shirley, wrapped in a white towel, ran into the room. She broke into tears immediately and took Little Alexander in her arms, crushing him tight against her chest. "I heard what you were saying." She held Little Alexander so forcefully he struggled to get away. "You'd rather kill us than have a family at all."

"We weren't going to do anything," Henry said. "We were playing."

"Boys are all the same. Always hurting something. Just once I wish one of you could feel half the pain I've had to go through."

Henry's mother and Uncle Dale appeared at the door. How awful things must have looked: Aunt Shirley crying as if the entire world had come down on her, clutching Little Alexander like he was her life-buoy and she wasn't ever letting go.

"The big one has a mean streak in him, and the little one does whatever he says!" Uncle Dale crouched down beside his wife, wrapping her and the child in his arms.

"They were going to suffocate Little Alexander," Shirley sobbed. "He was practically on the verge of death." Uncle Dale turned to his wife, assured her everything would be all right, and guided her and Little Alexander back to their room.

Henry's mother sat down at the desk and looked over the paper Henry'd been writing. He wanted her not to read it, only for her sake. His mother, Henry thought, had always been a kind woman, entirely reasonable, and Henry had worked so unusually hard to spare her more tears.

"You were making a list?" she asked.

"It's not fair that they get to do whatever they want," he said. He looked at his mother sitting in the chair that was entirely too small for her adult body. In her face, he could read the exhaustion that lurked under her eyes and which she hid with cover-up each morning before work.

"I'm really surprised at you two. You know we can use the rent money Dale and Shirley are paying us. Plus they're family, your father's family, however, but family nonetheless. They'd do the same for us. Your Aunt Shirley was a Godsend last year when your father ran."

"You mean 'didn't come back.' He didn't come back. There's a difference," Henry said. He slid into his bed and lay back into the fresh pillow, staring at the thick, zig-zagged wires supporting the bunkbed above him where Jess slept. Soon he lost all sense of anything else going on in the room, and only vaguely heard his mother say to Aunt Shirley later that evening that they'd be making the room-switch in the morning.

Immediately after breakfast, Henry and Jess tore across the backyard toward the cornfield. "If they want to move things so badly, they can move them themselves," Henry said. Jess was the first into the corn.

Halfway across the back lawn, Henry turned to look at the house, now completely covered with the noisily whispering creatures. He saw that their long silver bodies had filled out and matured even more during the night and now their black-hole mouths—that had become recently visible—seemed to eat directly at the sunlight filtering through the trees.

Since it was Saturday, Henry and Jess made off to Mr. Trout's Bait Shop. The shop was a small cinderblock building at the back of Mr. Trout's big white house, and he opened the shop on weekend mornings to sell nightcrawlers, mealworms, and tiny fishes that the bigger fish ate. Mr. Trout was a lawyer, but due to his last name, he thought it'd be funny to open a bait shop. He also sold aquarium fish that came in bright whites, golds and blues. Henry liked it there, early Saturday mornings, getting caught up in the talk and the warm smell of the Fisherman's Friend lozenges men rolled around the insides of their mouths as they spoke. Jess liked it, too, for the candy Mr. Trout sold. Sometimes Mr. Trout gave them free samples.

That morning, Henry knew he and Jess were a little late for the a.m. rush. Only one car was parked outside.

"Hurry up," Jess yelled. He threw open the spring-loaded door and went in. By the time Henry caught up, Jess was staring intently at a jar of gummi-worms.

"There's the other one," Mr. Trout said to Henry. Mr. Trout stood behind the counter: wiry and wearing gold-rimmed glasses.

In front of him, a man with a wide brown mustache and an orange hunting cap held a bag of three goldfish that'd tucked themselves into one corner of the bag. "Do you have an aquarium?" Henry asked.

"Nope," the man said. "These are for the pike. They really bite on these."

"You mean you're going to fish with them?"

The man nodded. Henry looked at Mr. Trout, and Mr. Trout put his hands in the air. "All I do is supply them. I can't control where they go."

"What are you two up to this morning?" Mr. Trout asked.

"We're going down to Black Bridge," Henry said. "My dad might be coming back that way from his special work with the FBI."

"Last week he'd decided to become a circus clown. You said he'd enrolled in the state clown college."

"He's talented at a great number of things."

"While you're there, if you two find minnows, catch them and bring them back here. I'll pay you ten cents for each one."

"We don't have a bucket," Henry said.

Mr. Trout produced one from behind the counter. "Make sure you return it."

"I'll be sure," Jess said, reaching out to touch one of the gummi-worms.

"You can have one," said Mr. Trout. "You, too, Henry." Jess slurped his down, while Henry held his in his hand, savoring it until he started to sweat and his hand turned red from the dye.

"Come here a minute," Mr. Trout said. He walked to the back of the shop where the aquarium fish were kept. Henry could see fancy goldfish and neon tetras and bug-eyed black moors. "Here's something I want to show you." Mr. Trout pointed to a large freshwater tanked filled with baby guppies. "You see that, there on the leaf?"

Henry looked closer. Jess already had his face as close he could go and was fogging up the glass. On a broad-leafed plant, a curious life was bobbing about in the aquarium's current. It looked to Henry like a small, almost transparent gray branch with tinier branches going out in all directions.

"That's called a hydra," Mr. Trout said. "I found him in there one day by accident."

"I read about hydras in my myth book," said Henry.

"It's like that. All those arms are like tiny mouths picking at food that floats by. And see that part there where it's all bloated? That means it's about ready to split, so instead of one head there, it'll grow two. That's how it gets bigger."

Jess soon lost interest in the stationary life and started pointing at the one goldfish he'd someday buy and name Goldie.

Henry, however, couldn't help watching the hydra a little longer. It reminded him of the strange things that had suddenly overrun the house, how they were not there one day but seemed to grow and multiply. He watched the small life pulsating in the water, increasing its size and the number of hungry mouths before him. "We'd better go," Henry said.

Mr. Trout handed the boys gummi-worms "for the road" and sealed them in a Ziplock bag. "So none get away," he said.

From Mr. Trout's bait shop, Henry shadowed Jess across a nearby wheatfield, coming eventually to the wall of blackberry briars that grew in thick between the river and field. Henry could hear the murmuring of water washing over rocks and the low purr from where the river fell several hundred feet just below Black Bridge.

"There it is," Jess said and pointed, before starting a path through the brambles.

Henry could see the high immobile structure that was Black Bridge jutting above the treetops. It was an old railroad bridge that kids would've been diving from, had one girl not broke her head open on a rock a few years before, he remembered. Against the green of the trees and the blue of the sky, the black of the bridge was a prominent skeleton; only the basic framework had been completed. Henry imagined it waiting for someone to color within the lines, and until that time, the sky and the trees would hold place.

Jess ran down to the water and began turning over rocks in search of minnows. He dredged the shallow pools with Mr. Trout's bucket, and his first attempt brought only a mayfly nymph and something that spun in circles.

"You should let me do that," Henry said, taking off his shoes. "I stand a better chance of making us more money than you do."

Jess dumped the bucket's contents and moved farther downstream.

Henry bent over his reflection in the water. All around him, he could smell the tangy drunken scent that came with August as the slower-moving river gradually revealed the more elevated sections of its riverbed. Along the opposite bank, a small marsh of trapped water had formed. Henry watched as a silent blue heron picked its way among the cattails and arrowgrass. It cocked its head back behind its shoulders, and then, like a crossbow, shot forward and into the water, piercing a fish with its beak. When Henry moved in the bird's direction, it didn't fly away as he expected. It watched him, instead, with caution.

Jess came running back with a bucketful of minnows. "See how many I caught?" Henry could count at least twenty, all small and wriggling in the red bucket.

"That'll make $2.00," Henry said. "Give me a try." He grabbed the bucket and waded farther out into the river. He decided to use just his hands, afraid some of those fish already caught would empty back into the water. He stopped at a shallow pool were a large school was corralled.

At first Henry came up with nothing. The tiny minnows flipped and wriggled between his fingers, slipping away safe and back into the water. They were still too little to be caught. Henry decided to re-strategize and stood up. He and Jess were both here that morning when their father said, "Old Russ has had enough of this for the day." Then he'd told them he was going home. But there was a car waiting on the other side of Black Bridge. Henry had not seen it, but now that he thought back, the sound he thought might've been thunder was the motor of a car. Instead of growing more and more faint with the distance, it had grown louder.

Nearby, Jess was building a small arena out of rocks, preparing to make crayfish battle one another as gladiators.

"I think if we stand here long enough, Dad might be coming back," Henry said. He looked at the far end of the bridge, and for a moment thought he saw someone standing there. It could have been his father—Henry could almost make out the beard and the large shoulders—but then it seemed to be the Amishman, stepped down from his wagon and dressed for a funeral. Then it seemed that it was no one at all.

"He could be coming any day now," Henry continued. "I have this feeling. Then Uncle Dale will have to move out."

Jess built the wall of the arena even higher.

"He said I was his sidekick. No one ever leaves a sidekick behind." Henry looked at the bucket with all the fish swimming in it, then turned to gauge his brother's response.

It came then. As a fast hazy gray, and he saw Jess launch it.

The rock struck Henry hard on the forehead. He yelled, not so much from the pain, but from the utter surprise as everything around him shifted suddenly and lost focus. Henry put his hand to his head, felt his legs weaken beneath him, and then he was sitting in water. The bucket overturned with a splash.

"Why do you have to keep talking?" he heard Jess say. And then Henry heard small footsteps splashing across rocks and water, and then Jess's angry complaints that soon became as muted as the footsteps themselves.

"Don't go. I'm all right," Henry said. He could hear water falling farther downstream. Then the flapping of a large bird's wings, rising above him.

"I won't tell anybody," Henry said. "I'm okay." But Jess was gone.

Henry could feel a numbness clouding the inside of his head, directly behind his eyes. It was heavy and full and ripe, and he held his hand to the gash on his forehead, wanting to keep the pain confined. Jess had changed everything, and Henry listened as all the sounds of the river—the hoots of the bitterns and the popping of water under rocks—quieted. *He saw it coming, a little beyond Black Bridge, moving just like the first day he'd seen it drift across the sky and lower itself over the house. But now, as it came nearer, it was somehow beautiful the way it caught the sunlight and threw it back in rainbows. He could feel the warmth emanating from it, even before the first of the smooth, wormlike bodies wrapped itself beneath his arms, around and between his legs, gently around his neck. He felt their slight weight, winding over his mouth and covering his nose. But he didn't struggle against them. There was an energy moving in each one—pulsing behind the pale blue eyes that were sad and empty and all so alike. He stopped wanting to move, and they carried him away.*

everything valuable
and portable

They decided to keep the book hidden, for safekeeping. Joan was eleven, the oldest, and suggested they hide it in her room, behind the guinea pig's aquarium. The others protested, accusing Joan of trying to keep it for herself. William suggested that they put it someplace where they could all enjoy it and share. The best spot seemed to be the bottom drawer of their mother's china cabinet, under the lace tablecloth and boxed set of silverware. Tucking it in safely, the children made sure no page was bent, that no part of the binding was crushed.

The first summer mornings, their mother allowed Joan to carefully lift the book from its secret spot and take it to the couch in the den. William and Lizzie squeezed in on either side of Joan, and Patrick, the youngest, sat on Joan's lap. The younger children listened as Joan read to them, turning the pages. The book began with a brief biography of the Virgin Mary and ended, on page thirty-four, with that of St. Boniface. Each page was devoted to an individual saint, some the children already knew of and others with histories more obscure. Each saint's description was accompanied by a picture, drawn large and painted in brilliant colors. After each morning's reading, the children decided which saint they'd choose to play that day.

All the children wanted to be St. Dorothy of Montau, a peasant who'd given birth to nine children and was the patron saint of young brides, difficult marriages, widows, those who'd lost infants to death. She prayed with her arms spread wide, in imitation of Christ on the cross, and died when her heart burst, unable to contain all of God's wondrous love. The accompanying artwork depicted St. Dorothy as a young, beautiful woman with golden hair. At the center of her green tunic was a red heart, from which streamed light, stars, and small swirls of rainbows, beaming out all around her. Joan and William argued over who got to be St. Dorothy, though it was inevitable that Joan, as the eldest and a girl, would get first choice. William resigned himself to Michael, the Archangel. Lizzie chose Rose of Lima, the saint of flowers, because Lizzie could barely get thoughts of flowers out of her head. Patrick decided on St. Francis of Assisi. William started calling him "St. Francis the Sissy," but Patrick, who wanted to be a farmer when he grew up, didn't mind because St. Francis watched over the animals.

Early on in this new game, William, Patrick, and Lizzie tried on different saints, thinking maybe Joan would give up her claim to St. Dorothy. "Nothing doing," Joan said. "I am St. Dorothy."

Then one morning Lizzie decided she was going to be St. Dorothy, too. She cut a heart out of red construction paper and pinned it to her T-shirt. She told Joan they could be twins—twin

St. Dorothys! Lizzie stood up on a chair with her arms spread wide, then she bent over Joan, pushing the construction paper heart into Joan's face like it was a flower for her to smell. Joan said she'd kill her before she let her be St. Dorothy too, snatching Lizzie's paper heart and ripping it to pieces.

After they finished with the book each morning, Joan stowed it back in the china cabinet—Lizzie smoothing the tablecloth over the top, Patrick patting down the box of silverware—then they went into the backyard, stomping at the edge of the pond, playing saints. Each day brought a new episode in the game, some new evil for them to battle. They imagined squinting-eyed swordsmen and hulking lion-beasts with horns growing out the top of their heads. Soon, they were seeing devils and demons that inhabited every square inch of their yard.

At war with these spirits, the children learned that prayers weren't unlike casting spells. With just a few words, with a pair of clasped hands held convincingly in front of your face (or raised triumphantly toward a cloud), the evils were dispelled, parting quickly but not without anguished howls the children could hear long after the demons were gone. Lizzie would often be captured. The demons wanted her beautiful flowers. And William, Joan, and Patrick crouched beside a large rock, drawing battle plans into pond clay while Lizzie screamed for help from a tree she hugged tight with her arms.

Their mother thought it would be fun to make costumes for the children. Money was short, but using old clothes, she set to work at her sewing machine. Joan held the book open to the specific pages, and their mother smiled and snipped with her shiny scissors. With the children's help, it took her all of one morning to make four costumes. For William, their mother took a white nightgown and added a pair of small wings (made from wire-hanger and nylons). Lizzie's dress was mix-and-match, swatches of bright colors stitched together. For Patrick, she sewed together their father's old brown hunting vest and allowed him to take a few of his stuffed animals outside.

Joan's costume was the most extravagant. Their mother found a mint green dress she'd worn as a girl and sewed a bright pink heart in the center of the chest. Joan decorated the edges of the heart with glitter and added trails of sparkles down the flowing sleeves.

"My four favorite saints," their mother said, as she took a snapshot. The children played until lunchtime, when she went out onto the deck and rang the tiny gold dinner bell. The children lifted their heads and went running for the kitchen.

At 4:30 every afternoon, thirty minutes before their father came home, their mother would call out, "Time's up!" and the children would dart for their rooms, urgently running through the house, Lizzie and Patrick screaming like their hair was on fire. The children slipped out of their costumes, returning them to their proper hangers in the hall closet.

Their father was no-nonsense and liked having things quiet once he got home. He was never angry or mean but would leave the room when the noise reached a certain level. More than anything, the children longed for his company and had learned, intuitively, how to please him. Hearing his car in the drive, their mother would rush to the bathroom mirror, to brush her hair or add lipstick. The children sprawled before the television in the den. If it was a good day, he would ask the children to tell him about their own; on bad days, he greeted the children with silence and Joan would hand over the remote, so their father could watch the news.

One particularly good day, their father came home singing. He had already removed his tie, and the top two buttons of his shirt were undone. Lying on the floor of the den, the children smiled at each other in anticipation. Earlier that afternoon, they had triumphed over a horrible three-headed mystery that had risen from the bottom of the pond and were eager to share in their father's good mood. Their mother brought everyone glasses of lemonade with straws.

"Have I ever told you kids how much I love your mother?" he said. He pointed the remote at their mother and pressed a button. "I want to pause her this way forever."

"I wish you could," said their mother. "Who needs more wrinkles?"

"Pause me, Daddy," Patrick shouted.

"I'll pause all of you," their father said, "even stuffy Joan, even myself. I'll keep us all this way for as long as we can stand it!"

They didn't visit Grammy's often, but when they did, the children and their mother would stay for a few days. Grammy was their maternal grandmother and lived three hours away in a condo north of Philadelphia and had a plump orange cat named Jupiter. Grammy's husband had died when Joan was just a baby. Two plastic flamingos were poised in Grammy's front lawn on either side of a birdbath. Every time their mother and the children would visit, Patrick said he felt sorry for the flamingos: they were so close together but unable to see each other because the birdbath was in the way. Lizzie liked throwing pennies into Grammy's birdbath. It was much better than the wishing well at the mall where, unable to retrieve her pennies, she could only get one wish at a time.

"How do you like the book I sent you?" Grammy asked. The children always spent the first ten minutes with Grammy before they were allowed to run wild through her neighborhood.

"We share it," Joan offered.

"Joan holds it all the time. She always holds it and she only lets Patrick turn the pages. She thinks it's her book," Lizzie complained.

"We've put it in a 'public' place," their mother said, picking a cherry from a bowl on Grammy's coffee table. Grammy always put out unsalted nuts for the children and a custard dish filled with cherries for their mother.

"When was the last time you took the children to Mass?" Grammy asked, tossing a pillow at Jupiter who was biting a leaf of her jade plant.

"It's been a while," replied their mother.

"Not since Christmas," Joan specified.

"Really?" their mother asked, surprised. "Has it been that long?"

"You should take the children. It's their right," stated Grammy.

"They find religion in their own ways," their mother suggested. "John gets so bored at church. He squirms worse than a child."

Grammy lit one of her thin cigarettes that smelled like candy. The smoke lifted up, branching out in wisps, smaller and smaller.

Jupiter wandered back to the jade plant. Grammy didn't notice. He bit off a thick waxy leaf and carried it with him to where he circled and lay under Grammy's chair.

Things hadn't been going well for their father at work. He called it "downsizing"—and then, something worse happened. The children and their mother had been visiting Grammy again. She'd taken them shopping at the mall in King of Prussia and out to lunch, and when they came home, the children carried their new purchases to their rooms. Suddenly, Patrick screamed from the den, and the other children ran to him. The TV was missing. And the VCR.

"We've been robbed!" yelled Lizzie.

"What's wrong?" asked their mother, coming from the kitchen.

"We've been robbed!"

Patrick started crying. William consoled him by petting his head.

"Quiet everyone," their mother demanded. "Everything's going to be fine. Let's check the rest of the house together."

They checked their mother's room; her jewelry was safe. The children ran to their rooms, to check on their toys, which all seemed to be accounted for. The guinea pig looked curiously from his bed of woodchips. Joan was sure he'd seen the robbers. "If only we could get him to talk," William said.

Then Lizzie remembered the book. Though they'd gone on to other games, the children still counted the book as one of their most treasured possessions. They all went scurrying to the dining room.

"The silver's gone," their mother said, disappointed, holding up the empty box for the children to see. "I'm calling your father."

On the phone with him, their mother twisted the phone cord around her index finger. Suddenly she froze. "I don't understand," she said. "I mean, I do understand, but . . ." As she placed the phone back into its cradle, she stared blankly, knitting together thoughts inside her head. "It's a mistake, children," she told them. "A terrible mistake."

"What's a mistake?" asked Lizzie, who had wrapped her arms around Joan's waist.

"There were no robbers, and there's nothing to worry about. The important thing is that we're all safe."

By the time their father came home, the children and their mother were sitting quietly in the den. The children were coloring, and their mother stared at the empty spot were the TV had been, had her hands crossed stiffly in her lap.

"I hope you're going to get everything back," said their mother, refusing to look at him.

"Back from where?" Lizzie asked.

"The repair shop," their father said. "I took some things in for repairs."

"Who broke the TV?" said Patrick.

"Yes, who did break the TV? And the silver?" their mother asked.

"I'm going upstairs," said their father.

He did not come down for dinner. In fact, the children did not see him at all for the rest of the evening.

The next day, their father came home from work with the TV, the VCR, and the missing silverware. "See!" their father said, showing them the shine of recently polished silver. "See, everything is good as new!"

Very quickly, things had become tight. Their mother said things weren't as bad as their father let on, but she made a point to only buy sale items at the grocery store. There were no longer allowances for unnecessary things. Their father bought lottery tickets, first the scratch-and-win kind that he'd let the children rub off, and when these failed to be winners, he went on to Lotto. Their mother found her Bible. It had been sandwiched between *Ivanhoe* and the world atlas on the bookshelf.

After dinner, while their father sat with his drink on the floor circling "help wanted" ads with a green pen, their mother would sit in the easy chair, turning the pages of her Bible.

"I want us to go to church this Sunday," their mother declared.

"Can we?" Joan asked. The children had only been to church a few times, mostly at Christmas and Easter, and sometimes with Grammy. They liked being with the kids their age in the Sunday School, learning fun things about the Bible while the adults learned the boring parts in Mass.

"You all go," their father said. "Sunday's one day I don't have to wear a tie."

"I want you to come," their mother said. "We've been having a lot of bad luck."

"Since when has luck been a Christian phenomenon?" their father said, in the voice he used when he wanted to show their mother how smart he still was.

"For me," she pleaded, staring at him, willing him to wilt under her pressure. "Okay, whatever," he said, giving in. "Whatever." He folded up the newspaper and threw it into the fireplace, even though there'd be no need for a fire anytime soon.

Come Sunday morning, their father regretted his commitment. He cut himself shaving and threw his razor into the sink where it clattered against the porcelain. Their mother tried livening things up. She made a big breakfast of fresh sticky buns and let William use butter, though he usually avoided dairy products. Their mother told their father how handsome he looked. She fixed his collar and smoothed down the part in his hair. "Don't get used to this," he said.

It had rained during the night, and Patrick ran his hand along the side of the car, splashing water at the girls.

"Stop that, Patrick," their mother said. "The girls look so pretty." Patrick splashed them again, and their father grabbed him by the shoulder.

The car smelled like their father's aftershave and their mother's perfume. Their mother held their father's hand while he drove. Sometimes he'd take his hand from hers to make a turn, but afterwards he put it back in their mother's lap.

At church, the girls straightened out their dresses and did everything their mother did. The boys went running up the steps. Lizzie pointed out the stained glass.

"I feel like everybody's staring at us," their father said.

"They're staring because you're so handsome," their mother said, taking their father's arm. William and Patrick had run ahead to find the best seat.

Lizzie wanted the family to have its own pew. Their mother was at one end, their father at the other, the children in between. The organ blasted so loudly it shook the church. The children could feel it humming up and down the pews, and Patrick covered his ears. "Don't do that," their mother said. "It's beautiful. Beautiful music." Patrick uncovered his ears for a moment and listened. Then he nodded.

Their mother was the only one in the family who knew the words to the service. Joan pretended she did; she listened to all the people around her and tried to mimic them, but she made a lot of mistakes. "You don't know it," Lizzie goaded. "Why are you saying it if you don't know it?" Joan's face turned red.

"Just try children, try," their mother instructed, and they did. They didn't say all the right words, but their mother whispered that it didn't matter. A man and two women in front of the family turned to look at the children, as their mother said, "God hears what's in your heart."

At the far end of the pew, their father kept silent. The children were surprised that he didn't know the words, either. He kept his arms crossed, rising and sitting, but refused to kneel. Their mother did everything in graceful motions. The slight angle of her hand set the charms on her bracelet ringing.

When it came time to pray, the children felt their mother's prayer must certainly be better than theirs. They asked for things like more toys, for their father to win the lottery. Lizzie said her prayer aloud until their mother corrected her with a tap on the head.

The collection plates began to be passed at the front of the church, sparkling under the lights. Their mother gave each of the children a dollar to contribute. William hated to give his dollar up. He kept all his money under his bed in an empty pickle jar.

When the ushers approached their row, their mother put in a twenty-dollar bill, then Patrick added his dollar, then Joan and Lizzie. Joan was afraid she'd drop the collection plate and spill all the money on the floor. She imagined how embarrassed she would be, crawling after the rolling quarters. Their mother smiled at each of the children, nodding as if they'd done a good deed. When the plate came to their father, he looked at it for a moment, then looked at their mother. Without a word, he reached in and removed their mother's twenty-dollar bill.

The usher seemed surprised, but passed the plate on to the next row. Witnessing what their father had done, their mother refused to acknowledge him for the rest of the service. "Why'd he do that?" Patrick whispered.

"Ask him on the way home," their mother replied.

But the car was silent on the way home. Their father tuned the radio to the sports station, as their mother looked out the window. The children knew to be quiet.

The rain started again, small drops falling against the windshield and chasing each other along the passenger windows, and their father clicked on the windshield wipers.

The Sunday paper lay on the doorstep, wrapped in a piece of blue plastic. Before their father could shut off the car, their mother got out and started up the walk.

"What's wrong with her?" their father said.

"Maybe she had to go to the bathroom real bad," Lizzie answered.

The house soon felt the way it had the day the TV had gone missing. Things were hushed, but not in the good way the children associated with the pine forest or lying on inner tubes in the middle of the pond.

The children watched the rain from the window of Joan's bedroom. Bright sun broke through the clouds and turned the surface of the pond to gold. From their bedroom, their mother and their father yelled. Then, suddenly, the house got very quiet. Joan, at the window, could see their father walking down from the house, toward the pond. He carried a plastic cup with him and sat on the large rock, the one the girls used to sunbathe. Their father's blonde hair was tousled by the wind. He slipped off his shirt and his shoes, tossed them behind him, and took a long drink from his cup.

Their mother came into Joan's room. She'd taken off what she'd worn to church, her dress and the charm bracelet. Her lipstick had come off her lower lip, making her mouth look swollen. A yellow barrette in the shape of a dog held back the hair on one side of her head.

"Lightning never strikes twice in the same place, right?" William said.

"Is it true?" Patrick asked. "If there's a thunderstorm, should I wait for lightning to strike somewhere and go stand in that place after so I don't get hit?"

"Yes," their mother answered. She looked dreamy and tired, like she'd spent the day in a high, windy place. "Yes, go stand where the lightning strikes. What's your father doing?"

"I think he's going for a swim," William said. "Come look."

"I don't want to look right now," their mother said. "Why don't you four give your father some company."

Lizzie looked out the window. "I think he wants to be alone."

"No he doesn't," she said. "I know your father." The children found their play shoes in the hall closet, went out onto the second-floor deck, and started slowly down the hill toward their father. No one wanted to go first, the mood their father must be in. They walked single file, Joan leading, taking soft whisper steps, ready to run at a moment's notice. Once they got close,

Joan held up her hand, and the others stopped. Their father rubbed his nose, making a snotty sound the children knew came when your head got too wet.

They climbed onto the boulder where their father was sitting. First Joan and Lizzie hugged him around the back, then William on one side, until finally Patrick pressed his face into their father's chest and the few tickling chest hairs. His skin was warm where they put their arms around him. "Thank you," their father said. His words smelled of whiskey, but the children squeezed tighter, and it seemed for just a moment that they, together, might be strong enough to lift him.

what are you afraid of?

The house in which Claire's parents lived was not a house but a hunting lodge. It sat among trees, smoke streamed from a chimney. It made you think of fairy tales, of grandmothers consumed in their beds by wolves.

Hartley didn't mind the drive. That was the lesser of evils. Trees along the Pennsylvania highways were covered with dazzling ice. As roads grew narrow and again more narrow, the ghost-face of a deer or rabbit would peer from snowdrifts before face and animal went skittering off. "Oh look it," Claire would say, jabbing her finger at the windowglass. Hartley, reluctant to shift his eyes from the road, nodded and patted his wife's hand. "You didn't see it," she said. "You didn't even look."

"Sure I did." He was going to be a father now, he kept telling himself. Her health and happiness should be his prime concern.

They stopped for gas in Sinking Springs. The radio said to expect freezing cold. Storefronts were iced over, looked condemned; it was Sunday. Thanksgiving decorations still hung from mailboxes.

"Get me some coffee?" Claire asked, heading for the restroom at the side of the station. She looked like a flightless cherub, her cheeks fattened, the wisps of her hair brought up into a loose bun on her head. The baby was due in three months. What was said about pregnant women being beautiful Hartley had never trusted until now, until Claire. "Decaf. Cream, no sugar."

"Anything else? We have a ways to go."

"Nothing now. We'll stop later on."

Hartley hated stopping later on. One stop. One start. Why make the drive longer? "Sure you don't want anything else?"

"No thanks. I'm sure I'll need to go again anyway."

Hartley pumped the gas, then got Claire her coffee. The slow-faced boy behind the counter was watching cartoons on a small black and white TV. "You'll all need to pay for using the bathroom," the kid said. He pointed to a sign BATHROOM 25¢ and nodded like an idiot. Hartley paid the quarter.

Hartley could see Claire settling back into the car's passenger seat, and he rounded the building to the restroom that smelled of burnt eggs. A brown stain reached down the white cinderblock wall from an air vent. Although a sign proclaimed NO SMOKING, Hartley lit up. He wasn't going to stand in the cold; Claire wouldn't let him smoke in the car. When an alarm went off, a high-pitched annoying damn thing, he tossed the lit cigarette into a corner and slammed out the door, grabbing the coffee cup.

"Thanks," Claire said. "Umm smells good."

"Thank the idiot," Hartley said, pointing to the attendant who'd left his place behind the gas station counter and was running toward the bathroom. Hartley started the car. Quickly Claire rolled down her window. "Thanks for the coffee," she yelled and waved. The idiot stopped, waved back, though he didn't seem to know why.

For the next two hours, Claire persisted in playing that silly game counting cows along the road. Hartley didn't need to pull over again—thank God—but by the time they reached the lane to her parents' home, Claire was ahead, forty-five cows to seven. "Better luck next time," she said.

"You always get the best of me."

"Practice, it takes practice."

"And practice makes perfect."

"Look: grandma and grandpa's land," Claire said to her stomach. She tried to sidle closer to the window, arched her back, pushed her rounded gut forward. "See? Trees, not concrete buildings," and she turned to Hartley and sneered, as if all of New York City were his fault.

Claire's parents lived atop a mountain ridge. Climbing their unpaved lane was slow at best. Thin ice clinging to dirt and rock threatened a slide into a tree, all the way down if brakes failed. Hartley was extra careful. He turned off the radio to give full attention. The tires missed once, stones loosened, whispering down the lane. The slope leveled, and Hartley could see that house—smoky, broken, miserable—squatted among trees. A dog the size of a small black bear ripped at its chain bolted near the front door.

"Just like I remember it," Claire said.

"It hasn't been that long."

"A year."

"A year, not a lifetime." Hartley parked the car in the drive so it was facing back the way they came.

"Daddy must be plowing again," Claire said. A plow-blade hooked to the front of a brown pick-up menaced from the side of the lane. Her father was fond of telling snowplow stories, how he intentionally tore up macadam one year because of those bastards at the road commission, how he'd saved a whole family who'd been stranded in the snow. He prided himself on his knowledge of roads and weather and how the two played off one another, made life treacherous for drivers.

The front door opened. Rena, Claire's mother, came onto the porch. She wore her trademark flannel shirt, too-tight jeans. Her hair was high and red, out of control, stuck uselessly with a plastic comb. At least Claire had some style, Hartley thought; she didn't insist on dressing like a hick, even if she was one at heart.

"It's Ruby," Hartley said. "Ruby Tuesday," and he was about to burst out singing, but Claire grabbed his wrist and dug in her nails.

"You think you're so smart," she said. "You're just afraid you'll actually like someone on this earth for once."

"Fuck off, Claire." Hartley grabbed her by the neck, kissing her, which always made her smile. She was so wonderful that way, living in a world of touch and touching. When he first met her, through a friend of a friend of a friend, the only way people of unlike backgrounds could possibly ever meet, he'd thought of her first in terms of touch. She'd been visiting the city and he'd noticed how uncomfortable she seemed, the look of helplessness about her, to which Hartley was unusually predisposed. Helplessness was rare among the women he knew. Such a wonderful trait lost to the modern age.

By the porch, Rena managed to settle the bear-dog. Its strong black head pressed under her hand. The dog's name was Sarge, Corporal, Captain was it? Something to do with war.

"Please be good," said Claire.

"Whatever else could I be?"

"I'll let you answer that."

"Be careful," Hartley said, but she'd already slammed the door, was headed for Rena's widely spread arms. Icicles dropped like daggers from the house's awning, shattering on the harder, icier ground. Rena kissed Claire on both cheeks, then longer on the mouth. Hartley shut off the engine, took a deep breath. And away we go.

"Hi ya," Rena said. "Thought you were going to sit in there with the motor running." Hartley couldn't decide whether or not to lock the car; it'd become second nature. "Who do you think's gonna steal that way up here?" Rena asked.

"Just a habit."

"Come inside you two before my grandson freezes to death."

"Or granddaughter," Hartley corrected.

"Grandson. Pease women have sons first," said Rena, rubbing her hand across Claire's stomach as if it were a crystal ball. Claire was no longer a Pease woman, he wanted to tell Rena. That name had fallen, disappeared completely when he'd taken Claire as his wife. She'd risen, ascended, transcended this place.

Rena gave Hartley her usual crushing hug, digging her fingers into his back. These were the same fingers he'd stare at, remarking how easily they deboned chicken, pried envelopes open faster than a knife.

The bear-dog let out a low, guttural rumbling when Hartley stepped onto the porch. Its fangs were just bumps now, hidden under loose drapes of mouth skin. "Nice dog," Hartley said.

"Don't mind General. He's over-protective."

"Just doing his job, huh?"

"Come in, come in," Rena said. "We've been waiting."

The kitchen was warm and damp and smelled of chestnuts. Rena confessed the log walls weren't the best insulation. Christmas music blasted from speakers hung by wire rigging over the kitchen sink. *Fall on your knees, O hear the angel voices.* Christmas was still three weeks away. In one corner of the kitchen, the black deaths of flies clung to flypaper. "I've made some muffins," Rena said. "Apricot. Just about to take them out of the oven." Rena inverted the muffin pan onto a gingham cloth. The muffins seemed oily, too wet.

"Where's Daddy?" Claire asked. She squeezed between sink and kitchen table and tried to suck her stomach in, but it didn't budge.

"Your daddy's in the other room. Go say, 'Hey.' I'm just finished here."

Hartley hated to leave Rena, but he wasn't about to leave Claire, so he followed her into the living room. Bob, Claire's father, was bent over a table made from a sheet of plyboard and two sawhorses. He was prepping a ruffed grouse, considered himself a taxidermist. The living room was taken up by several dead and stuffed animals: deer, fish, owls, squirrels. They seemed happy staring from their perches.

"Hey, there's my girl."

"You look as young as last time," Claire said, pushing her face into his chest. She could be such a liar. Bob was sixty-five and looked it. You could tell he'd once been a man other men might've feared, but now he was thin, striated, only bones. He moved slowly and carefully. Hartley disliked him.

"There's the professor." Bob looked over Claire's shoulder, and though Bob was smiling, Hartley never felt comforted.

"We had such a nice drive," Claire said. She petted the ruffed grouse, as if it were alive, capable of appreciating her attention. Bob set two marble eyes into the dry sockets of the bird's head.

"How's your health, Bob?" Hartley asked.

"Do you like my grouse? I call her Bisby. Why? you ask. Because I do."

"Such silly names for things," Claire said. "Isn't that silly Hartley?"

"Sure, silly."

Hartley sat on the edge of the sofa. Rena had covered it with rainbow afghans, three at least, overlapping. She'd made them herself, was crazy about afghans. Cold as it was, Hartley wanted to wrap himself up in one. Fire crackled and expired in the fireplace, but it didn't throw out much heat. Small black wisps went swirling up the chimney. This was getting back to nature.

Hartley kept a suspicious eye on the stuffed and the dead decorating the room: the pensive twelve-point, the bowing moose. He thought of those cartoons that showed the rest of the animal standing, hidden, behind walls.

"So how's the professor?"

"Doing just fine, Bob." A fat yellow cat crawled against Hartley's leg, rolled onto its back showing its white-tipped paws. Hartley reached down to rub it, but the cat hissed and darted under a magazine rack stacked full of *Reader's Digests*.

"Written any good books lately?"

"Oh, maybe one or two. It's hard to tell."

"Don't be modest," Claire said. "Tell him about the award."

"No, it wasn't—"

"It was a major award," Claire said. She stripped her sweater overhead and sat beside Hartley on the sofa. He took her hand that was soft and limp and comforting.

"It wasn't that major—"

"Get any money with it?" Bob asked. "That's what I want to know." He righted the grouse onto a mounting board, angling the bird's head so the grouse seemed to be pecking, taking aim at insects among dry elderberry grass.

"No," Hartley said, "No money with that one."

"Sometimes it's just an honor to win," said Claire.

"A person likes to win." Bob kept his attention fixed on mounting the grouse. "I guess that's why I hunt."

Hartley leaned into Claire's shoulder, she squeezed his hand, and for a second he wished he could crawl right into her, disappear into her soft flesh and forget he'd ever written any stupidly intelligent book on Joyce's *portmanteau*. Another book to add to the fodder, another reason to keep librarians busy, shelving books nobody'd read unless they were writing their own books about books nobody'd ever read. Hartley's books, all five of them, were held in the university library. Secretly, he'd visit them, take the elevator to the tenth floor where he'd walk casually up and down the long and shaded and tomblike rows. The air was suffocated with dust, heat vents rattled when Hartley clicked on the overhead lights. He'd pause, surprised almost, to find his books on the shelves, among so many others. From time to time, he'd sign one of them out, just to keep them in circulation, just to have them stamped, giving the impression of use and usefulness.

"You're breaking out in sweat," Claire said.

"Too hot? I'll crank the flue open. That'll let some heat out." Bob started toward the fireplace.

"No, actually I'm cold," Hartley said. "I don't know why I'm sweating."

"Don't get sick," Claire said. "We have a long drive home."

Lunch passed. Hartley was thankful he and Claire decided not to visit a week before, for Thanksgiving. Bob and Rena were enough without Claire's older brother and two younger sisters and their screaming, fighting brood. Claire was the last to "bear fruit," Rena made known. Bob said he would've put his money on Claire to be the first one knocked up. Not that she was a wild girl; she'd just always seemed to choose eager young men. "But what can you do when love comes? That changes everything," Bob sighed.

"What did take you two so long?" Rena asked.

Hartley looked into the bowl of peas. "Just waiting for the right time."

"The right time for what?"

"The right time for us," Claire said. "Sure it's easy for you guys to want grandkids. You wouldn't have to live with them all the time." Hartley nuzzled Claire's foot under the table. There were times, few but important times, when her sense of loyalty amazed him. She'd married him for better or worse.

Hartley ate to avoid talking. Rena kept passing plates, plate after plate, filling with turkey and water-clear gravy, yams and pecan pears, string beans with wild mushroom sauce, pig souse and pickled-beet eggs. Hartley liked Rena's cooking, though with each bite, he was sure of the lard, of the things he'd learned were lipids and cholesterol that were now entering him, buying him extra time at the gym. Claire talked about baby names; she was infatuated with the idea of having the power to decide a name. "Like Adam and Eve," she said. Bob huffed—he didn't believe in the Bible—yet he admitted not wanting to miss out on Christmas and Easter. Rena talked of the things that occupied her life: cooking, shadowing Bob. Hartley nodded. If conversation stopped, Hartley asked to be passed something. Nothing could be more important to Bob and Rena Pease than more good food.

After the meal, Hartley followed Bob into the living room, Claire trailed her mother into the kitchen. Hartley had offered to help clear the dishes, but in the Pease house, tradition was tradition.

"You two relax," Rena told him. "Men relax. Women work." Relax from what? Hartley wondered. For what?

Bob didn't talk at first but went to finishing the ruffed grouse. Hartley hovered close, this meant interest, feigned at least, and he'd lean toward Bob or nod at what seemed proper moments. Against the windows, snow and ice pelted, slicked the glass.

Everything outside looked on the border of night, though it was only past one in the afternoon.

"I like that turkey over there." Hartley pointed to a corner of the living room at a large angry tom turkey, puffed full of air, its tail flared. "Did we have him for lunch?"

Bob looked up, took a red handkerchief from his pocket and slathered his nose. "Nah, that one I got a long time ago. What we had for lunch Rena bought. Turkeys she doesn't trust eating wild. Deer steak, rabbit, Rena doesn't mind, but wild turkey, she says the taste disagrees with her. Wild tastes different than tame. You know the difference?"

"Don't think so."

"Well, when you've tasted wild, you know it. Tangy right in the muscle."

Hartley could hear the women in the kitchen, laughing. Plates clattered, slid into stacked place. "Well, that's one fine bird." Bob pulled a pack of cigarettes from his pocket, offered one to Hartley. "I have my own," Hartley said. The second after, he wished he'd taken one.

A scratching, a shuffling came from the back patio. Hartley turned, looked at the sliding glass door on the opposite end of the room. Bob looked up, too. It was Will, Claire's brother. He and his wife lived on a neighboring ridge, in a house not unlike Bob and Rena's. Will toted a gun, barrel pointed at the floor. Stepping inside, he shook his thick locks, sending snow and sleet and iced water spraying. Snow melted and dripped from his full and poorly trimmed mustache.

"Hey, the professor's here," he said. "How ya doing, professor?"

"Pretty good. And yourself?"

"Can't complain. Came over to see if Dad wanted to do some shooting. The weather's a bitch, but I got targets set up over my place. Hartley, you shoot?"

"Not much. It's been a while."

"Dad and me will teach you. You should know how to shoot."

"I don't know how much shooting I'll do, but I'll follow along," Bob said.

"Just let me tell Claire—"

"They'll figure it out," Will said. He wiped off the gun, rifle, Hartley wasn't sure exactly what to call it. He knew there was a difference. One was definitely wrong. "Grab your coats, gentlemen. We have some damage to do."

The icy rain slacked off. Trees looked brittle, new. Hartley took each step at its time, placed each foot surely and solidly. He couldn't risk tumbling down the side of the mountain.

Will had set up styrofoam targets, bull's eyes, one each on six strict elms along the ridge connecting his place with Bob and Rena's.

"You want to go first, professor?" Will asked.

"Why don't you show us how it's done," Bob nodded.

"First things first." Will bent over, fished behind a pile of split firewood, brushing leaves and snow from a half-empty bottle of whiskey.

"You still have that hid out here?" Bob asked.

"Have to keep it from Merla. She'd finish it." Will took a drink and passed the bottle to Hartley. The bottle felt right. Hartley was no stranger to drink. He'd promised to cut back. How long had it been since he'd had whiskey? Hartley drank as deep and long as Will, then passed the bottle to Bob.

"No thanks. That stuff's for the young."

Will took another drink and set the bottle at his feet before taking aim at one of the targets. Hartley kept an eye on him, trying to memorize his movements. The last time Hartley held a gun of any sort had to be when he was a kid, something his father had tried to show him at the club, shooting clay pigeons. At the time, Hartley had shown no interest. He'd planned on buying his food from a supermarket, not foraging for it in the woods.

Will pulled the trigger. A loud crack shot up then splintered down through the valleys, breaking and breaking and breaking again. "I think you got that one dead center," Bob said.

"Run up and look." Will meant for Hartley. Hartley took another slug of whiskey. "Don't worry, I'm not gonna shoot you."

"Course not," Hartley said and jogged across the snow. Halfway to the target, he remembered the ice, tried to slow himself down, but the sudden shift made him slip, almost fall. He grabbed onto a low branch. Ice crinkled.

"Yeah, you got it. Straight on."

"Told you so," Will shouted back. "Step out of the way. I'll shoot again." Will prepped, took aim, spread his legs like a batter squaring up to take a pitch. Hartley sidestepped a couple feet, didn't want to inch too far away, didn't want to seem too mistrustful. "You can stop right there. I'm not going to hit you." Will smiled and nodded. "Yet."

Another crack, this time near center, almost perfect. "Good shot," Hartley yelled. He hurried back across the icefield toward Bob and Will who was drinking the whiskey. Hartley swiped the bottle from him.

"Your turn," Will said. He handed over the rifle, it was cold, Hartley wished he'd had the sense to wear gloves. He took another swig of the whiskey, shouldered the rifle, stopped, took another swig of the whiskey, shouldered the rifle, aimed, and pulled the trigger. The rifle kicked, but Hartley stood ground. Will hurried, crazy-legged, skidding across the snow to the target. It was clear Will had been drinking long before uncovering that whiskey bottle. "Pretty good shot. Take another."

Wait 'til he moves out of the way, Hartley told himself. *Wait 'til he moves.* Will ducked behind a tree, but he was so big his shoulders and arms couldn't be hidden. "Yoo-hoo," Will called. "Don't shoot me." Hartley took aim again, this time throwing the bullet a little more to the left, a little bit farther from where Will was acting crazy behind the tree. The shot hit the target at least. Hartley hadn't embarrassed himself completely.

The sleet came again, persistent and heavy. It slipped down through the trees, humming, mechanical almost, it wouldn't stop. Bob covered his head. "I'm headed indoors," he said. "My old bones can't take it."

"Me and the professor's gonna stay here." Will sauntered back from the targets, threw his arm over Hartley's shoulder. "Those targets aren't quite full of holes yet."

The sleet came harder and then disappeared completely, the gray clouds exhausted. Hartley and Will finished off the bottle. When it was empty, Will turned it upside down, acting surprised there was nothing left. "I guess we're two big drinkers."

"Lots of practice."

"Me too. Drinking and hunting, my two favorite hobbies. You're pretty good for a city boy."

"Drinker?"

"Shooter." Will tipped the gun against the woodpile. He got himself a log and sat down, stretching his long legs into the snow. In the Pease house, lights flared on, upstairs, downstairs. On through the trees, Hartley could make out the similarly golden windows of Will's house. "See what you're missing out here? Take a load off." Will hit a space beside him on the ground. Hartley grabbed a log from the pile and sat. The whiskey was doing the trick. The ice didn't bother him a bit.

"It is nice, I guess."

"You guess? Sure it is. I couldn't live anywhere else on earth."

It felt good to sit. Hartley settled into the wood, the air smelled fresh, clean, pure, the way things should be? Maybe this was how other men felt all the time? Here in the woods, concerned with things that concerned men—shooting and drinking, drinking and shooting. Now Hartley felt included in this circle of men.

"When you joined the family," Will started, "we had you pegged as the black sheep. Hartley the Hardly, that's what Dad and Mom were calling you. You didn't know this, of course, and I wouldn't be telling it to you if I didn't like you. It's like, now, you're one of us."

Hartley smiled, kicked at the snow. *This is something I'll be bothered by later*, he thought, but for now, he let Will clamor on. Will got up, walked behind the woodpile, started pissing on a tree. "No peeking," he said.

"None of that from me."

"Just joking. We never thought that," Will said. "But you're all right. Even old Bob's taken to you, and that's like leading flies to water."

Through the trees, back toward Bob and Rena's house, Claire came onto the porch. She had a quilt, some blanket wrapped over her shoulder. She'd finally given way to the cold. "Come on, Hartley. Let's start back. Hey, Will? How ya doing?"

"Great to see ya Sis. Try visiting again in the next two or three years."

"We're so busy in the city."

"That's not what your husband's been telling me."

"You can't believe everything you hear. Come on, Hartley, let's go."

Claire went back inside. Hartley couldn't think of anything more perfect than Claire, how she called to him, wanting him to come to her.

Will slapped Hartley's leg. "You got yourself lucky, my man." Will wiped a trail of chew oozing from his mouth. "Claire's a looker."

"Yeah, sure is. Why do you think I married her?" Hartley laughed.

"Why's a man marry at all." They both laughed at that, then Will stopped short, staring down into the valley. Hartley saw nothing but trees and trees and a sheer rock cliff. A deserted road turned in and out of places. "Yep, Claire's a looker. When she was twelve, thirteen, I used to sneak into her room when she was sleeping. The prettiest thing you'd ever want to see." Will spit, rubbed his red nose. "I don't think she ever knew about it. I didn't wake her, but I could get myself so close, just inches away, I could smell her . . ."

For a moment, Hartley entertained disbelief: he'd not heard what he heard. He stared into the valley, its quick slopes, the jagged spires of its trees. *Canyon*, he suddenly thought. It was more like a canyon than a valley, its sharp edges obvious now under the covering of trees. He looked at the rifle that'd slid into the snow, then looked again at the canyon, back to the rifle. Pick it up, he was telling himself, pick up the rifle and take that son of a bitch's head off, right here, right here in the snow. He could imagine Will kneeling by Claire's bed, the perfect impropriety of it, Will's large body leering close to Claire's sleeping one. Pick up the rifle, Hartley was telling himself, pick it up. His finger twitched. Then nothing. Though anger was everywhere in him, Hartley couldn't funnel it, couldn't make it at all useful.

Will threw his arm over Hartley's shoulder. "Thanks for spending the afternoon with me, professor."

Rena had wrapped things to take back to the city: leftovers, muffins, things she'd knitted for the new baby boy. Hartley went through the motions: hugging, thanking, turning, hugging, thanking. He felt liquid and loose. He wouldn't go back into that house.

Claire bundled herself tight in a scarf, ran to her mother and father and kissed them like a child leaving on a long interminable voyage. She wrapped her arms around Will, Will with his shaggy head and unkempt mustache that scuttled her neck. "I'll miss you most of all, big brother."

"Come on, Claire. You wanted to go, let's go." Hartley honked, started the engine, the exhaust purred. By the house, at the end of its chain, the bear-dog was leaping, yelping excitedly, looking both happy and neglected.

"Wait a second," Bob said. He held up his finger, went inside. He returned carrying that stuffed turkey, the proud prancer Hartley had noticed earlier in the corner of the living room. "Professor, I want you to have this."

Hartley looked at the bird, its shiny and deep black rainbow feathers, its taut red head and purpled skin dangling over its beak.

"Oh Dad I don't know if it goes with our apartment," Claire said. She looked worried, teasing a finger in her hair.

"Put it in the back, Dad," Hartley said.

"There's a man speaking." Hartley saw how happy that made all of them—all of them except Claire—him letting Bob put that turkey in the back of the car. Bob crossed a seatbelt over the bird. "In case of accidents."

"Can't be too safe," said Hartley.

Good-byes said and done, Hartley urged the car down the mountain ridge, toward the highway. Claire put the heat on full blast and kept turning back, looking out the window, waving.

Along the highway, large fallen branches glistened white in what was left of the sunlight. "They look like hands," said Claire.

Hartley kept an eye on the turkey in the backseat, how it jostled against the seatbelt when the car took a turn or went over a bumpy patch of road. It looked angry and blurred, its red head and ruffled skin, its black eyes, its stiff neck.

"Watch where you're going," Claire said. "You're over the line."

Hartley veered the car to its proper lane. "I know how to drive."

"Just stay on your side."

"Stop it, Claire."

"I was just saying—"

"Stop it."

"Hartley—"

In front of them, the road opened up, around a curve, to where you could see for miles, out into the same valley maybe, same canyon Hartley and Will had looked into before. Hartley swerved to the side of the road. The front of the car scraped the guardrail.

"What? What happened?" Claire screamed. She had her hands crossed on her stomach, shielding herself.

The motor still running, Hartley jumped from the car, threw open the door to the backseat, and grabbed the turkey by its neck. It felt scaly and wet, stiff like a weapon. Hartley didn't care about ice, about slipping, about snow and ice and slipping. Clutching the turkey, he charged at the guardrail and flung the turkey out, into the open air. It seemed to hang there for a second, like it might just take to flight, fly off into the horrible orange sun. But quickly the bird sank; it was too heavy to hang longer than that second. It grew smaller and smaller as it fell, a fact that now amazed Hartley as the turkey landed first against rock and then disappeared into the black of thick pine trees.

"I don't want that damn thing, I don't want it," Hartley yelled. There was no echo. Nothing out there to answer but empty space.

He turned back to the car. Claire had risen from her seat, stood shielded now behind the passenger-side door. She cradled her stomach in her arms, locked hands. She looked lost, confused. Hartley thought he'd the power to save her, and yet now, he was seeing her really, honestly, for the first time.

"What the hell are you doing? You've been drinking?"

"Claire," he said.

"You could've gotten us killed, number one."

"I don't want that thing. I just don't want it. Please understand." He could feel Claire staring at him, trying to figure things out.

"Why'd you take it if all you were going to do was throw it away?"

"Do you know what Will told me? When he and I were shooting?"

"How could I know? I wasn't even there."

"Will told me he used to sneak into the room when you were sleeping and lie next to you."

"So what?" Claire said. "He and I were very close."

"It was the way he told me," Hartley said. "Something wasn't right."

"You think you're so smart when it comes to me. Always," she said. "I wasn't sleeping." she said.

"You weren't?"

"I knew it all along." Claire braced herself by the guardrail, looking out into the canyon. Strands of hair had loosened from her bun and eclipsed her ears. "The attention was nice. It's not what you're thinking, but it was nice."

Hartley slid into the car. He tried his foot on the accelerator. With just enough pressure, he figured he could send them—him, Claire, the baby—all of them right through the guardrail, send them out into the open air, where the tires would keep spinning, trying to find leverage, the motor would still be running, purring, and they'd hang there, midair for just that second, before starting to fall.

It was getting dark now. Claire got in beside him. "The front of the car's smashed," she said. "Who knows what kind of damage you've done. I hope we can make it home. Anyway, don't talk to me. Don't even try to talk to me about this. You'll ruin it by talking about it."

"It's okay. Don't worry," Hartley was telling himself.

"And get out of the car. I'm driving."

"Everything's okay," Hartley said. The radio crackled, went in and out of range. Somebody out there was trying to get through.

second-hand

My father doesn't want to watch, so he stays on the screened-in porch with his book of word-finds. Sue and I wait for him to settle before starting with the big dresser bureau. The top drawer holds nylons, lingerie, delicate items rolled into balls. My sister and I take them out, unfold them, unball them, fold them again and put them into piles on my father's bed. During this drawer, my sister and I don't speak. These were Mom's private things she'd be embarrassed to know we are touching, even though Sue and I both are fast approaching thirty and now have families of our own. This drawer would also be the most painful for my father, I imagine. What secrets and desires each piece of sheer clothing must have held for him, when my mother was alive and their room was sleepy and dark.

Next we find Mom's tops and blouses. My sister holds a few against her chest, to see if anything might be her size. "We should get rid of it all," I say.

"You're right."

I can't picture my sister wanting to wear any of Mom's clothes anyway. My mother's things were never new, always used, bought second-hand from thrift shops and yard sales or passed on to her by our more well-to-do neighbors. With Mom, every penny went for me and Sue, for college, for us to have nice things. She'd always believed spending money on clothing, on herself, was a waste.

Sue and I tackle the third and fourth drawers: jeans and slacks, still neatly pressed. I fold out a pair of green corduroys. For a moment, my sister and I stare, as if we're expecting the empty legs to suddenly fill and dance like they did, drunk or sober, at St. Patrick's Day parties, spinning Mom around the room, making everyone laugh.

"This isn't going to take as much time as I thought," my sister says. She fingers the raspberry birthmark above her left eyebrow, her comfort spot, something Mom managed to trick Sue into believing made her more special and more beautiful than all the other girls in her kindergarten class. "If we get this done quick, maybe it won't hurt as much."

"Maybe," I say. "But what if hurt is what we need?" We look at each other, silently for just a moment, and then turn quickly away, as if we've been caught looking too long at our own selves.

In the closet we find Mom's dresses, the same she wore to PTA, sports awards banquets, church, graduations. There are surprisingly few: a rose floral print, a canvas safari-dress, a black one with white polka dots, one of sleek red-foil with a bow at the rear. We pull out jackets and the scarves, Mom's housecoat, her few pairs of shoes and throw all of them onto the empty corner of the bed.

There's only one thing left to do: Sue and I pick up the black garbage bags from the floor and place the clothes inside, careful not to disrupt the piles and folds we've made. I don't know why we're being so cautious. Maybe it's because Mom was always so careful; she protected and treated everything, our furniture, our lawnmower, even our cars as if they were frightened wet birds, delicate and precious things.

Mom's clothing fills two bags total that Sue and I tie and sling over our backs. We carry the bags into the kitchen and stop for lemonade; we've broken a sweat, it's so hot. "Dad, we're finished," I yell to him on the porch.

The glass door slides open. My father's face looks like a knot: lumpy and wrinkled, barely holding itself together. "No trouble?" he asks.

"None," says my sister. My father stands in front of us, staring at the two black bags of clothing, everything that came near to her skin. I feel the weight of these black bags, too. Sue and I've put them down, aren't holding them at all, but they feel heavy enough to put a hole through the floor, sending all three of us into the basement.

My sister and I drive the clothes to the Salvation Army. It's what Mom would've wanted. This Salvation Army store is the biggest I've ever seen. It's inside an old supermarket, and in aisles marked CEREAL or INTERNATIONAL FOODS, you find instead worn children's clothing or ripped paperbacks. At the door, a man with a hearing aid tells us to leave the bags with him. "I'll take care of 'em," he says.

Sue and I look at one another. We're reluctant to let these things go.

"These are nice clothes," my sister tells the man. "You should put high prices on them."

"Yes," I say. "High prices."

"Loreen will take care of that," he tells us, as if we know Loreen and she's someone important in our lives. He's noticed my sister and I are still holding on to the bags, so he takes them and tosses them into an empty grocery cart. "I'll get these off your hands," he says.

My sister returns to her own family the next day, but I decide to stay for a while with my father. Leaving, Sue wears a pink summer scarf tied loosely about her neck. We walk her to the car, telling her to drive safely, to obey the speed limit. When she's gone, my father and I find we have all and nothing to say to one another. We have dinner at T. G. I. Friday's and talk about the food.

At night, lying in my childhood bed, I hear Dad moving about his room, opening and closing drawers. Sue and I tried to fill them out with his things—his shirts and pants, underwear, socks—but even with his clothes in them, the drawers seemed empty. I'm sure this is what he's thinking too, as he's trying to calm himself down for the night, so he can possibly get some sleep.

I'm driving past the Salvation Army the next morning, so I stop, just to be sure. I go piece by piece through the racks of used clothing and find nothing that belongs to my mother. I know every donation is washed first before being released into the store, so it takes two more days and two more visits until I find some of her things: the dresses. They seem so different here among the strange pieces of clothing.

I wander up and down the aisles, keeping my eye on the rack that holds her things. Several women pause at them, lingering long enough to examine a hem or finger a button, but each time, the hangers fall back into place, the dresses unknown and unimportant among the other second-hand clothes.

When no one is nearby, I stand in front of my mother's things, looking at them, touching them as if the grooves and creases in the fabric are some private language, some braille my fingers will read and remember. I think of all the threads, tightly entwined.

I'm not sure how long I wait.

At the end of the aisle, a woman with a ponytail fishes through the racks. She has silver rings on all of her fingers, and the skin on her face is taut, drawn back over her severe cheeks and up to her forehead. She looks permanently tired and drags two small girls behind her, their hair ratted and messed, almost as if it's never been brushed. One of the girls carries a green plastic sand-pail, using it as a purse. The other one, whose eyes look too close together, holds onto her mother's leg.

The woman comes toward me, moving in stops and starts, pulling dresses between her long fingers, stroking the fabrics, sometimes holding clothes up to her body. When she nears my mother's dresses, I stand back and watch. She passes over the canvas one, the red one with a bow. It's the black one with white polka dots that gets her attention. Growing up, I secretly hated this dress. Whenever Mom wore it, I'd find reasons—a water fountain, a floor-plan, an interesting stain—to keep me on the opposite side of whatever room she and I happened to be stuck in together.

The woman with the ponytail takes hold of the dress, looks under the sleeves, making sure there are no hidden rips or tears or loose threads. She takes it from the rack, lays it out in front of her so she can get a good look. The girl with the plastic pail tugs on her mother's sleeve. "Wait a minute," the mother says, returning the dress to the rack, pushing it in, almost lost among the others.

She continues down the row, but even though she's moved on, she keeps looking back. I know she's thinking about my mother's dress, assessing its worth. Both girls are clutching onto the woman's leg now, vying for the same space. "Stop it," the woman says; she has to tap the kids on their heads to get them to let go. Then she stops and returns to my mother's dress, takes it from the rack. Again she pulls at the fabric, turns under the hem. She makes a slight noise, a note of consideration, scrunches her nose as if about to sneeze. Then I watch her fold the dress carefully over her arm.

"My mother used to have a dress like that," I say. I can't help it. It comes out like that. To make matters worse, I must be smiling.

The woman stares at me, her face even more drawn and now surprised. "Really?" she says. I realize how odd I must seem, a man standing alone in the middle of the dress aisle at the Salvation Army.

"You'll like it," I tell the woman and quickly walk away. I don't want her to chicken out, to put the dress back, so I leave and wait outside in my father's car. I don't turn on the radio. I don't roll the window down. I listen to myself breathe.

Fourteen minutes later, the woman with her two children comes carrying a small shopping bag. The three of them climb into a corn-colored Buick; it's old and rusted and reminds me of the one my family used to have before we had nice things. I watch the woman buckle her kids in for safety. She does a loop in the parking lot, her turn signal blinks good-bye at the stoplight, I see the tops of the children's heads, and she leaves.

When I go back into the store, down the racks of dresses to where the ones belonging to my mother hang, the black and white dress is gone. I've never been prone to tears, but now they would somehow feel right, complete and unshaming, but I don't cry. I'm too proud.

"Can I help you with something?" a woman's old voice asks. I turn. Her hair is high and white with streaks of blonde, looking like a cloud's touched softly down on her head. I stare at her, memorizing her face, all her perfect imperfections. "I'm sorry, sir, but can I help you find something?" she asks again, impatient this time.

"No, probably not," I tell her. "But thanks for asking."

life among the bulrushes

T he one named April is the first to go.
Daniel Peale collects the brown caterpillars that have slipped
from their spidery tents in the wild-cherry trees and gives them
names of people he knows and doesn't particularly like—names
belonging to the smiling schoolmates of his ninth-grade class,
names of distant relations, names of TV stars. Standing over
the small fire he's built on the dry shore of the backyard pond,
he plucks the plump caterpillars one at a time from a Tupperware bowl. He lets the one named April drop into the fire.
Flames catch the tiny hairs on her back. April shrinks and
shrinks and disappears.

Before he drops each caterpillar, Daniel speaks its name
aloud: Patrick, Cousin Michael, Sandra Bullock, Barb, Jenny

Jones. If any of the caterpillars manage to escape—perhaps by a gust of wind or bad aim that sends it far from the fire—Daniel will let those go. If Mrs. Peale interrupts in the middle of this judgment as she often does, Daniel will also let the caterpillars go. He's convinced moments such as these, small and unexpected triumphs, are moments of truth, intervention, and faith, designed elsewhere by powers he could only hope to challenge.

This time, the one named Patrick is blessed enough to miss the fire completely. Jenny Jones, however, isn't as fortunate but drags herself somehow from the flames. Daniel watches the two survivors crawl slowly off, moving away from the heat. He licks his fingers before killing the fire with dripping-wet handfuls of pond clay.

Inside the house, Mrs. Peale is preparing for the trip to Ocean City, shoving clean and dirty clothes into duffel bags. She's packed the styrofoam cooler with grape soda pop and Budweiser. When Daniel comes into the living room, holding the empty Tupperware bowl, Mrs. Peale straightens and raises a cigarette to her mouth. "I told you about using my good plastic," she says. Daniel shrugs and tosses the bowl onto a pile of dirty clothes. He knows Mrs. Peale takes every opportunity to make him feel younger than he is. When she looks at him, he's sure she doesn't see a fourteen-year-old with long legs and big arms and promising thick black stubble. Instead, she sees only the boyish cowlick, his light unaging eyes, and the silver braces along his top row of teeth that Daniel blames her for not taking care of years ago, when others his age were going through the same thing. Only at nights is he free to become who he has wanted to become full-time. He'll reconsider wrestling practices, the head coach who also teaches physical science and suits up in the same locker row. A force like that of God has stood next to him, naked, revealed, a body made purely of moss on rocks. Daniel volunteers for a demonstration, the Fireman's Carry, his body up-ended and mouth stretched as his face meets the foam mat, a weight as if the whole world has violently seized him, only to whisper, warm-breathed and with sincerity, "Mine," into his ear.

"We're leaving in the early morning," Mrs. Peale tells him.

Daniel knows this, has known it for weeks. He won't be going with his foster parents, Mr. and Mrs. Peale, but will stay home to look after the grandmother. Referring to the Peales, Daniel doesn't use words like *Mother* and *Father* because these words sound wholesome to his ears and imply connection. He likes to imagine that his true parents—the one man and one woman who united and made him and whose last name is something other than Peale—are dead. They died possibly in a horrible collision/explosion soon after his birth. He's told himself this story so many times that he's come to believe it.

Daniel knows why he was brought here thirteen years ago to live with the Peales: Barb Peale is *barren*. No matter how hard Sam huffs and puffs, there's no hope for his wife. Some nights, the gypsy moths bump against the window screen, and Daniel pictures Sam and Barb, grunting and prostrate like animals, foolishly hoping for something to take hold and grow.

Daniel's on his way to the backyard shed to fetch beach chairs when he spies Grandma Peale sitting on the screened-in summer porch. "Urgugurh," she utters. Since her stroke four years ago, Baba's been confined to a wheelchair and the whims of her son and daughter-in-law. Wherever they choose to leave her is where she remains. Most often she can be found in a corner of the porch overlooking the pond, staring at one point in the distance. Before the stroke, she'd been a real presence, and in Daniel's mind, the glowing ember in the dying light of the old house.

He remembers the time, in a religious fit, that Baba had gone about the house nailing crosses above every door and smearing raspberry preserves—convinced it was a form of ram's blood—

alongside every jamb. He was only eight years old and how excited he was to hold the jar for her as she dipped into it again and again with the table knife! Small blobs of the preserves had oozed onto his hand, and he licked at them, holding the tart delicious flavor in his mouth as he followed her from room to room. He'd lie on the goose-down comforter at the foot of Baba's bed while she'd read silently from her black Bible. The light on the bedside table was just enough to keep the room from falling into that still uncertain darkness of night. Mouthing scripture silently to herself, Baba would touch her forefinger to her tongue before turning each page and only speak when she'd come across a particularly important passage. Then, her eyes would grow larger, an "Ah-ha" would slip from her, and Daniel, suddenly alert, moved closer, staring at her as words on a page transformed to truth. John 3:16. Matthew 7:1. Mark 16:16. *He that believeth and is baptized shall be saved; but he that believeth not shall be damned.* First Peter 1:7. *The trial of your faith, being much more precious than of gold that perisheth, though it be tried with fire, might be found unto praise and honour and glory at the appearing of Jesus Christ.* She made Daniel commit these verses to his head—over and over again like songs that lodge themselves in memory—and would reward him with pear candies or allow him to select a beautiful button from her sewing box. She warned Daniel not to fall into the same ignorance to which her son and daughter-in-law had so unfortunately committed themselves, a world of material things and present-day, a world entirely closed off to divine grace and guidance. Nights like this, a yellow brilliance waved from Baba's eyes. He almost feared her, for she gazed so intensely, as if she really could see that slight yet troublesome pillbug of disbelief scuttling about inside him. Before switching off the tablelamp, she'd tug on Daniel's ear affectionately and make him recite her favorite: Matthew 9:22. *Daughter, be of good comfort, thy faith hath made thee whole.* Daniel's lips would still be poised in the circle of the final word when Baba would smile and fall back into her pillow, closing her eyes as if sleep had come that suddenly.

Sam and Barb have never thought officially to remove the crucifixes that Baba put above the doors—there's certainly too much effort involved in sliding a stepladder to each one. Some have loosened themselves naturally, however, and if made of glass or porcelain, have broken to pieces on the hard floor. For so long, Baba was convinced an angel was coming to carry her away. This was all before that day four years ago, when staring into a cat's-eye marble she'd plucked from the decorative jar atop the refrigerator, Baba Peale closed her eyes, counted to ten, and had a stroke. Since then she's been unable to utter a word. Only short pieces of sound pass from her mouth. Though it's quite possible these sounds are a jumble of intelligence, no one can understand her. He's reluctant to believe that her talk about the bright light of God, about the passage from life to death to eternal life, has ceased. When he looks at her sometimes, at the thin gray hair clinging tenaciously to her pink scalp, Daniel catches glimpses of what Baba used to be peeking furtively from behind those eyes.

The backyard pond rests under a layer of mist. Mosquitoes and fat swamp-flies skim the surface, lowering their heavy abdomens to the water and expelling eggs. The swamp water is green-gray and oily. A small rowboat that children might pole to the middle of the pond sits on the shore. Hidden amid beggar-weed and swampgrass, frogs twitter, calling to one another. It's a softer version of the voices that speak to Daniel during the night, reaching out like warm hands from the dark center of the pond. And now, the way Baba continues her unintelligible sounds makes it seem that she's calling back to them.

Daniel cannot get over Baba's patience. The time he'd crucified a dead bird, the time he'd lowered a banana spider into the ant farm, any time he'd tested the tenuous thread between life and death, Baba was the only one to look past his behavior. She believed his testing a good thing as long as he showed faith and fear of the Lord. Daniel knows that Barb and Sam have discussed often in soft voices whether or not they should return him to where he came from, to maybe let him try another foster home. In recent years though, Sam's started making excuses for Daniel's behavior. Sam says it's hormones. Barb says it's run-off from nearby Three Mile Island that's gotten into Daniel's skin and makes him act so, though she adds that he's always had way above average test scores. The existence of these, excelling in one area and failing miserably in another, confounds her.

Barb's calling from the other side of the house, yelling, always, as if her leg's caught in a clamp-trap. Daniel remembers the lawnchairs he's supposed to be finding in the garden shed and carries them to the front of the house. Barb drags a suitcase along the walk, with three duffel bags slung over her right arm. She chooses to appear as the martyr. "Help me load the car," she says.

"Why don't we wait until Sam gets home?"

"Because our vacation starts at 5:00 p.m. For all of us, whether you're going or not."

"You're not going anywhere until tomorrow morning."

"Doesn't matter when we're going. It's a state of mind." Daniel knows Barb's fond of slipping things in like that, finding some way of tying the physical world to the mental at every opportunity. She thinks it makes her sound smart and modern.

It takes six more trips to and from the house to load the station wagon. Daniel carries the Coleman coolers, a bulging suitcase, the beach umbrella, a hot-air popcorn popper. When it seems they might be running out of room, Barb decides they should unload everything and try again. "There's got to be some way to make it work."

While Daniel unpacks and repacks the car, Barb leans under a red maple with a glass of lemonade. Daniel sees her look once at the whispering tents of caterpillars that have invaded the tree. She points, as if to object to their presence, but remains quiet.

Later Daniel thinks things have finally worked out until Barb comes from the house carrying three inflated beachballs. A sudden wind takes her by surprise and sends one of the balls blowing about the front yard. "Oh, no," Barb says, the way Daniel has heard her say it when finding a pot of water boiled over or a page in her trade paperback dog-eared.

Barb chases after the runaway ball, going, Daniel thinks, with the zeal of a child hunting Easter eggs. He thinks how unfortunate she looks: her thin brown hair flying into her face and open mouth as she runs. When she stops to retrieve the lost ball, the other two somehow escape her. Every time she goes running toward them, she kicks them by mistake. The harder she tries, the farther they seem to go.

"Help me get these," she yells.

It doesn't take Daniel long to rescue the balls. But once he's done it, Barb discovers there's no more room for them in the car. "I spent all morning blowing them up," she says and looks as if she's going to cry.

"You need to let some air out."

"No. There's got to be a way." She pushes two of them through a side window where there's little space. The plastic moans. Daniel waits, expecting the balls to pop, but they don't. Barb stops to wipe sweat from her face, then puts her hands on her hips.

There's the sound of gravel, and when Daniel and Barb look, a car has pulled into the drive. A large woman gets out, carrying with her a leather case. She's wearing a thin dress patterned with brilliant orange and pink flowers—blossoms both opened and closed—that remind Daniel of morning glories the way they climb and seem to wrap themselves around the woman's body. A straw hat is balanced perfectly level on the woman's head. She's smiling too much, Daniel thinks. Her pale, round face is unblemished except for a circular scar by her mouth that stretches itself bigger the more the woman smiles.

"Hello, neighbors," the woman says.

"Oh, no," Barb's immediate reply. Daniel remembers then that Barb and this woman have had run-ins before.

"Pardon me?" the woman says.

"Can't you see we're ready to make a trip? Can't you see that?"

"I can see that very clearly, Ma'am. If you'd only give me a moment—"

Barb grips the beach ball in one hand, meaning to do damage. "We don't need any Witnesses," she says. "You can take your brain-washing somewhere else."

"If you could give me one moment to tell you about—"

"No, thank you." Barb starts toward the house, still holding the beach ball.

"Perhaps the young man here thinks differently. He's old enough to make choices for himself." The woman's noticed Daniel staring at her. He's not so much interested in what she has to say as he is in her being on the front lawn. He takes it as a sign.

Barb grabs Daniel by the shirt. "Come inside. These people don't know when to quit."

"You're doing a great disservice to that young man by forcing deaf ears upon him."

"I'll take a pair of those deaf ears for myself," Barb yells back, slamming the front door.

The fat woman does not move from the front yard. She stands firm and immobile, like the lighthouse she believes she is. "Go away," Barb yells from behind the living room curtain. "We don't want you around here. Get out of my yard or I'll call the police."

Daniel and Barb watch the woman approach the house. She's come down the walk, up the front steps. She rings the doorbell. Daniel admires her persistence.

"I'm warning you," Barb yells.

The fat woman rings the bell again and again. It has become, in a way, a game.

Barb goes into the kitchen and comes back with a golf putter of Sam's. She opens the front door and waves the golf club like a flag.

"I warned you. We're not interested."

"Well," says the woman. "The Lord led me here for a reason. I can only go so far."

"You can go on in your car. What's the name of your person in charge anyway? That's who I'm going to call. What's his name?"

"You should know him as God," the woman says. She crams the leather portfolio deep into the crook of her arm and does an about-face, walking down the drive.

Barb doesn't go away from the front window until she's sure the woman has gone, then flops down on the living room sofa that lets out a sigh of dust. She stares at the ceiling fan whirring overhead. It wobbles and is missing one of the propellers. Daniel thinks the whole thing could fall at any moment.

Barb takes a deep breath and lets her hand droop over the edge of the couch. "Why don't you go get me an ice water?"

When it's that time of day for her to be indoors, Baba lets her head roll to the side like a weak-necked doll and leaves a trail of drool spilling from her mouth. Daniel pushes her to the living room, into the corner beside the clock where the comings and goings of her wheelchair have managed to keep a square of floor free of dust.

Sam gets home from work at the post office where he's postmaster and changes into Bermuda trunks and a T-shirt. He doesn't look like a postmaster but a college professor, with his gray beard and shiny head. He opens a can of beer and raises it in a toast. "To vacation," he says. He smiles at Daniel, like they're brothers. When Sam speaks to Daniel in private, sometimes sitting on the edge of Daniel's bed and smelling of drink, Sam likes to use the words *respect*, *trust*, *faith*, and *honesty* in talking about his relationship to Daniel. Daniel usually waits for Sam to kiss him good-night before rolling over to face the wall.

Now that Baba's in her corner, the Peales and Daniel have dinner at the Sinking Springs Family Restaurant. The walls are decorated with charcoal drawings of wild game. A stuffed deer greets patrons at the door.

"You wouldn't believe how much misdirected mail there is," Sam says, poking his knife at the air. "Today I counted fifty. And you would think it's because people move on, their mail gets lost, but the truth is people just aren't careful enough."

"Have another roll," Barb tells Daniel, pushing the small wicker breadbasket at him.

"You have to be careful with addresses. A simple mistake, just forgetting one number, one small thing, can mess up the whole system."

The waitress, whose name is Debbi, asks if they need anything else.

"We're going on a trip," Sam informs her. Daniel dislikes Sam's habit of telling complete strangers about his business.

"Oh, I wish I could go on a trip. I bet this young fella is going to have himself a summer romance." Debbi pats Daniel on the shoulder and when he smiles at her and says, "I'm not going," she draws back.

"It should be a wonderful trip," Barb's saying. "Ocean City is such a magical place. We're meeting my sister and her kids there. We go there every year."

Daniel can remember all the thirteen summers he's lived with the Peales as one because there's been little variation. They stay at a place called Misty Harbours that's at least ten minutes' walk from the beach. They each lie, unprotected in the sun, until their skins turn red so they can complain about sunburn for the rest of the trip. They get their pictures taken as a group by gamey camera boys who roam the beach flattering girls and making small talk with the adults but who don't think to look at him and smile. Barb Peale always agrees to the photographs, but when the time comes, they never go to pick up the photos and pay. That makes at least thirteen photographs of the Peales: lost, probably destroyed, never to be seen again.

It's as if the black earth has risen up and surrounded the house. There is no moon and the night is cold and nothing seems to exist beyond the windowscreen except for the sound. Daniel hears Barb and Sam leave when the clock reads 4:00 A.M. It's a six-hour drive through boring Pennsylvania countryside and cramped New Jersey, and Barb and Sam want to get to Ocean City in time to spend the entire day at the beach. Daniel hears the departing station wagon, imagines the red brakelights flickering at the end of the driveway before the car turns onto the road.

He sits up. Even in the dark, his feet find the floor.

Grandma Peale lies at the center of her bed, curled like a fetus, and murmurs from troubled sleep. Now Daniel realizes how very small she is, how much she has diminished over the years. He slides one arm beneath her neck, the other under her legs, and lifts. She's a bundle of sticks. Her eyes open. "Don't worry," Daniel says. Baba starts to mutter, slow and sleepily. Daniel remembers how she used to speak of black nights such as this as a time when the spirit of the Lord would possess the house and watch over every one of them. She'd tell the story as if the spirit were a wave and a flood with no hope of escaping its goodness.

Maneuvering Baba through her bedroom door is easy, down the carpeted stairs that let no sound escape, onto the porch. She doesn't struggle. Outside, Baba in his arms, Daniel doesn't bother to lock the door. He hears it slam shut behind him. That's enough.

He looks at the pond and sees it in a new way. Once the pond was declared DEAD by the State. For that year it was a HEALTH HAZARD and was glossed over with a slick, impenetrable sheen. Fish floated stiffly to the surface, and for days there was the noisy cackle of wayward seagulls picking at the dead. Then the birds were gone. Then not even a single crayfish scuttled between rocks. The year after, however, things cleared; if you looked hard, you could see new life: waterboatmen, gadfly nymphs, snails sliding over the black muck still clinging to the bulrushes. And now—not long from sunrise—voices of frogs and even spring-peepers have settled. Daniel feels conviction at this renewal of life and the revisiting of sounds to the pond. There is this new life pulled from death.

He lowers Baba into the rowboat and pushes it from the shore. He doesn't mind if he gets wet. Baba's sleeping again, peacefully now. He poles the boat toward the center of the pond. There have never been oars as long as he can remember. Only a long, unwieldy pole to push into the mud and move the boat slowly around the pond. The rowboat's movements make patches of thick algae pulse like hearts.

Daniel has read the story of Moses, thinks it, in a way, the most important story of his own life. This is one reason he feels that he and Baba are one: they are both abandoned, like infant Moses cast among the reeds. And in that story, Moses was found, and saved; he grew and prospered. Until Moses let himself be seized by faith and belief, he doubted God's intentions, questioned Him. With the appearance of the burning bush, however, God's love and Moses' love of that love were soon indisputable, inescapable.

Daniel looks at Baba sleeping. It's possible she knows what's going on. Daniel likes this idea that she knows, that he's not alone in knowing.

In spring there would be a slight current here, running just beneath the surface toward the end of the pond away from the house where there's a small stream, a rivulet Sam calls it, that only flows when the water is high. The heat's lowered the level considerably, and here, the deepest point, is only ten feet.

The Peales will be gone for eight days. They will not check in with him for at least four. He has made sure of this. It has to do with that thing *trust* he and Sam have discussed. Sam says that he *trusts* Daniel as long as Daniel promises to call in an emergency and no parties. Daniel promised, and this made Sam smile and admit he was so happy.

Daniel's given himself these four days to be touched by a higher power, to discover there's more to his life's plan than serving as foster son to Sam and Barb Peale. Surely God will show himself and complete the ring of Daniel's faith, filling in that one still questioning piece just as He did for Moses. Daniel's made rules for himself which include staying in the boat and doing without food or water. The same is true for Baba. Moses was provided for, and Daniel expects similar provisions. If for some reason the boat comes into contact with shore, he will pole it to the center of the pond again. He knows he will recognize God's presence when he sees it. It can come in many forms, he supposes, though he must be careful to keep to these rules he has set for himself. If this hasn't happened within the four days—the time limit he's given himself—he knows what must happen—and additionally what has happened—to him and Baba.

Looking at the house sitting like a blister on the dry yellow grass, Daniel squats in the boat and thinks: Yes, I will test God.

By afternoon, Daniel has rolled all of his clothing into a tight ball and wedged it into the prow of the boat. He is entertained by the appeal of his own body, the jut of his hip bones. The sun is unrelenting. He's undressed Baba to that point just before indecency. A white bra clings to her shriveled breasts. Her underwear reveals a slight circular stain, now dry. Daniel looks at her skin, at the thick blue veins pushing dangerously close to the surface. A scar in the shape of a frown—from a gall bladder operation long ago—stretches just below Baba's navel. It looks raw, as if it's never healed properly, though Daniel knows this can't be true. He's about to touch it, but draws his hand back, sticking his fingers into his mouth, touching them instead with his tongue.

Since getting into the rowboat, Baba has been quiet. He watches her stomach rise and fall. The scar stays a frown, moving between *more* and *less* severe.

Only once does the boat drift in any direction, and even before the temptation of shore can be a threat, Daniel poles back to center. Baba lies on her side. Her lips move and she sometimes blows bubbles.

Already he can feel the sun tightening and reddening his skin. He looks at the water all around him. Even though the deeper parts blend into numerous shades of blue and onward to black, he thinks it must be warm, from being caught in such a small warm place. He won't touch it. Not even when he feels thirsty does he move toward water. He tries to sleep in order to avoid the heat.

Around evening, around the time Daniel thinks it must be evening, he watches the red circle on the horizon. He stares at it, as if waiting on a clock, wanting it to move faster, to fast-forward time.

Male dragonflies slide against one another, jockeying for territory, crossing like swords. He sees at the edge of the pond, near a cluster of cattails, small black shapes that slip silently into the water and disappear. They could be muskrats, diving terns, something he does not know. He keeps expecting one of them to surface by the boat. He looks down into the water, sees nothing but his own face, and watches the sun again.

It's night. Baba tries to move. Daniel sees her tiny body reach toward water, but he pulls her back. He's much stronger than she is. When he looks into her eyes, saying "No, Baba, this is for us," he sees a tear and rubs it away with his thumb.

Even though the night is cooler, his skin's still warm from the day. He doesn't need a shirt, though he dresses Baba again. He watches her finger trace the wood patterns along the side of the boat.

When his stomach growls it reminds him of all the frogs, now emerging from daytime hiding to chirp and disrupt the night and keep him company. The moon this night is only a piece of the whole. But still it makes the pond look like it's lit with a swimming pool's submerged light. His head's so weary he thinks for a moment the light's coming from inside the earth.

Twice during the night Daniel wakes to the sound of wings. Twice his eyes open expecting angels. Twice he closes them to sleep again.

The second day Daniel begins to think that maybe Sam and Barb, for some reason, are on their way home. Perhaps one of them's forgotten something. Perhaps they've heard voices in their sleep and decided something is wrong.

Daniel thinks that it's an important thing to be loved, and if the Peales, Sam and Barb, do in fact love him and Baba, they will come. He imagines love works that way: it's an invisible wire between people so the slightest tug can be felt miles away.

When Baba starts crying, he kisses her on the forehead, and says, "I love you."

There is a slightness to Daniel's head. The smallest movement, the most insignificant sound captures his attention all through the second night. Gurgles and pops begin just beneath Baba's chest. Her face has turned bright red from the sun, though he's tried to protect her with his own body, his own shirt.

This night he tells her about three wonderful orphans who wound up not so alone because of their faith and persistence. During the story of Orphan Annie, Daniel thinks he sees Baba laugh. "Yes, that is a funny one," he says. "A very funny one. Imagine: a man named Punjab."

He's still laughing when he realizes that she's asleep.

He takes to praying. He feels tired and his head is light and the skin covering him is bright pink and parched and ready to flake.

He thinks now how it is, this thin flimsy line between life and death, this line that divides yet unites. His understanding began years before when he smashed a housefly in his hand and took the time to look closely at its lifeless body. One moment the fly was moving, the next it was reduced to a small wet jumble of parts. When the spirit dies, the body dies, yet if the body dies first, the spirit surely lives on.

Daniel sits, twirling the pole in his hands. Baba doesn't move much anymore. He lays the pole across the boat and slides his hand to the naked flesh of her stomach. He pats her there, mean-ing *everything will be okay*. He finds himself caressing the jagged scar just under her navel. He traces the arcing path with his fin-gertips and changes direction when he has come to one end.

He doesn't know whether it's night or day. Light has become something he's forgotten, though he's watching a group of ducks chase each other around the edge of the swamp. He half sees them, for they soon lose their shape and become colors. "Baba," he says. "Look." He turns her head so her eyes face that direction. Her head rolls effortlessly back into place. He's thinking about the next day, tomorrow, when it'll be time to enter the water, to feel its desired coolness finally wash over him. His test of God will be complete, and he will not be the one who's failed.

Now Daniel notices for the first time the woman floating down the small sloping yard to the shore. She stands with her hand raised to the level of her eyes. She looks large from the center of the pond and is wearing a hat and a brightly colored dress. "Hello," the woman calls out. Her voice sounds muffled, much farther away and unreal. She starts waving her thick arms. He cannot be sure, but Daniel thinks he can make out flowers— orange, pink, and fuchsia flowers—their large petals curving and reaching one over the other toward sunlight, or is it toward the heat rising from the water's gray surface?

"Young man," the woman calls.

She glimmers and fades, glimmers again.

"Young man."

Daniel feels words crawl to his lips, towing themselves through him, up and down and through him, until there's no part left untouched. His head barely propped on the edge of the boat, he smells the yellow decay lifting from the water. "Here," Daniel calls. This time louder, "We're here."